MILES TO RUN BEFORE I SLEEP

Sumedha Mahajan was born in the beautiful town of Amritsar, home of The Golden Temple. She is a business woman, runner, motivational speaker and writer. She is founder and CEO of business strategy firm Karta Business Consulting. She is married and currently lives in Mumbai.

For more information please visit www.sumedhamahajan.com.

In Appreciation

'Sumedha is an extraordinary person who has shown what perseverance and hard work can achieve. For someone born with asthma to run 1500 km tells us that when the mind is clear about a goal, however impossible it may seem, a person's determination can help attain that goal. My compliments to her for even dreaming of such a challenge and then achieving it. I'm sure that the book will inspire many and also prove that our women are second to none.'

—Milkha Singh

MILES TO RUN BEFORE I SLEEP

how an ordinary woman ran an extraordinary distance

Sumedha Mahajan

RUPA

First published by
Rupa Publications India Pvt. Ltd 2015
7/16, Ansari Road, Daryaganj
New Delhi 110002

Sales centres:
Allahabad Bengaluru Chennai
Hyderabad Jaipur Kathmandu
Kolkata Mumbai

ISBN: 978-81-291-3546-9

First impression 2015

10 9 8 7 6 5 4 3 2 1

Printed at Thomson Press India Ltd, Faridabad.

See yourself in mirror,
Remember your battles,
Remember how you stood against all the odds,
Remember your tears,
Remember how you picked yourself up when everyone was pushing you down,
It was you and only you, who made it through,
You are an inspiration,
Improve yourself and work on yourself so that you can aspire for bigger things.

I dedicate this book to all those brave people who broke the chains and followed their dreams and to those people waiting to get inspired to break their shackles and follow their dreams.

'Om Sri Sainathaya Namaha'

Contents

Prologue

I woke up late—excited, confused and scared. An opportunity of a lifetime had presented itself to me. I had made up my mind. All that remained to be done was making that dreaded phone call to my family and seek their permission.

I dialled my father. It was 7 a.m. and I knew by this time Papa would probably be in the middle of a lawn tennis game when I called him. But I desperately wanted him to answer my call; I would take it as a sign for me to pursue my dream.

And he did pick up the phone.

For a moment, it felt as though the air had been sucked out of my lungs. I mumbled, 'Hello, Papa. I hope I didn't disturb you in the middle of your game?'

He sounded as though he was in a good mood.'Just finished the set. We won. You called me just at the right time. So, how was your meeting yesterday with Milind?'

My father was obviously clueless about what had happened

to me in the last twenty-four hours.

'Papa,' I began with trepidation, 'something strange happened yesterday. Milind Soman invited me to join him and his team to run from Delhi to Mumbai.'

'That sounds interesting! But what are you going to run for? How many people are joining you guys?'

My heart skipped a beat. Did he just say yes? And was I worried for nothing?

I replied, 'It is a run for promoting a healthy lifestyle and to save the environment. There will be four guys and two girls, and out of those two girls one is going to be me.'

'Strange! Why such a small team? I hope you guys are running the campaign in a car. Ask your husband to join you, too. You guys could take your own car; it will give you more privacy and space. So, when are you planning to do it?'

My heart sank.

'Papa, you're getting it wrong. Milind Soman has asked me to run...physically run from Delhi to Mumbai in thirty days. It's a marathon meant to raise awareness about the environment.'

'Have you lost your mind? Delhi to Mumbai? Is this some sort of a joke? And your work, your family? Chinu, it's time for you to run around a baby, not around cities in these marathons that could damage your knees!' And then, just as abruptly, he said, 'My next game is up,' and disconnected.

It was no better with my mother. But I felt strangely stronger, calmer, after the disastrous conversation with my father.

'You've just recovered from an injury, Chinu, and yet you want to run 1,500 km now! You are twenty-eight years old and you already have too many health issues. You need to have a baby before it's too late,' my mother pleaded.

'Mama, I am perfectly fine. I'm strong and I know I can do it. I can plan a baby after the run. It's only going to be for a month,' I reasoned.

'Does Arvind agree to this? Have the both of you lost your minds?' she raised her voice.

'We had a detailed discussion last night...we decided together that I should go for this run.'

'Then why are you asking us? Go run!' she snapped.

'Mama, you know I cannot do this without your approval. A media company will cover the event and I will be taken good care of... Once I have kids I can never run like this. Please say yes and give me your blessings...'

'Will they pay you?'

'I'm not running for money, Mama, but for myself. Just imagine, I will be running with some of the best amateur runners in the country. This is huge, Mama. It has never been attempted in our country. I cannot donate money but I will give my sweat and soul to it and I'm sure it will all be worth it.'

My mother was quiet for a long time before replying coldly, 'You don't know what you are doing. You are immature and if you don't get your act right, you will ruin your family life. For once think about the consequences. You will be paying a lot more than just sweat and soul in this run.' She disconnected the phone abruptly. Her words remained in my mind for quite some time and my excitement turned into sorrow. Now I was even more worried and scared about my decision.

My sister, my best friend, just fourteen months older than me, had always been the protective and caring one. When we were younger, she was the one who always rescued me from bullies and helped me with my homework. She shared everything with me and always stood by me in whatever I decided to do. She knew me better than anyone. I turned to her for support.

She heard me out and she, too, slammed the phone down.

My younger brother was the only silver lining of the gloomy day. 'Awesome, Sis! Just make us proud. Chak De!' he almost shrieked on the phone. It was enough to make me smile, and this time, the tears were happy ones.

It was 5 April 2012. We were supposed to start in just twelve days. I needed to run at least 30 km for seven days and that too, in the afternoons, so that my body got used to the heat and humidity. With hardly any time left for me to prepare, my husband and I decided to go to Shirdi, to seek Sai Baba's blessings. I am an ardent devotee of Baba and could never think of taking up a challenge this enormous without any sort of sign from him.

We drove down from Mumbai the following Saturday for Sai Baba's *darshan*. Unfortunately, it was unusually crowded and they closed the gates early. I was gutted. It was the first time that I had come to Baba's shrine and couldn't get his *darshan*.

Was Baba annoyed with me? Should I look upon it as a sign?

I started doubting my decision. I sat outside his shrine so that I could get a glimpse of his face, even from a distance. I spoke to him like a daughter, and asked for his forgiveness if I had ever hurt him or others around me and begged him to show me a sign of approval.

But nothing happened. Eventually, we started our drive back to Mumbai. In just a few minutes I broke down completely. My husband knew I had to fight my own demons and I was glad he understood. He stopped at a deserted stretch and requested me to get out of the car. He led the way and we walked into a barren field circled by the Western Ghats. As I sat there, praying, weeping, not saying a word, my husband held me tight.

We must have sat there for an hour when suddenly, two egrets flew down and perched on a rock just a few metres away from us. It seemed as though they were looking at me intently, as though they could look into my very soul and discover my innermost desires. And they were telling me to follow my heart. I saw my sign. I looked at my husband and said, 'Let's do it.'

I wanted to create history. I did. Six people set a record by running 1,500 km in thirty days. And I was the lone woman who battled insurmountable odds to complete the race.

1.

Defective Piece

I AM NOT supposed to run.

I was born asthmatic in the historically significant town of Amritsar, which was untouched by modernization but witness to a bloodbath that eventually changed the destiny of the nation.

When I was growing up, the air was still fresh, unpolluted. The only people who typically had asthma were the elderly. During my early school days, my classmates, in ignorance and fear, shied away from me, as though asthma was contagious. During lunch breaks nobody came up to me to chat or play or even eat lunch. I was left out of their world. But I wasn't angry with them. I knew they were taught to stay away from ailing people. And in their eyes, I was always sick.

This discrimination was not limited to school. Even though my mother was a doctor and my family repeatedly assured all the kids that I was safe to play with, I still had very few friends. Some of my cousins, family friends' kids always looked upon me with pity: 'You are suffering because you are paying for your bad karmas of your past life. We know no one will marry you…you are always sick, you cough like our grandmother.' They called me 'defective piece' and 'dadima'. The only people who were good to me were my family and a handful of family friends.

At the time when children ought to be busy picking up new games and making friends, I was picking up survival tips from other asthmatic patients. I was mostly indoors, when other kids were out playing. The inhaler was my constant companion. My parents tried every possible conventional and unconventional treatment, discussed my condition with friends who had experience with asthmatic people and gathered information on how to take precautions. Their smiling faces never betrayed their angst and unhappiness about my condition.

During the harvest season, my condition invariably aggravated. I spent sleepless nights, long hours at hospitals, where the air would be heavy with dread and misery and the corridors and rooms crowded with dying people, ill people, weak people. My fear and loathing of hospitals go back to those miserable times.

I was rebellious and irritable all the time. I disliked people nursing and taking care of me. I wanted to break free, I wanted to be trusted and treated as an adult, like my older sister. At night, I would sometimes raise my fist in the air and ask God,

'Why me?' I never did get any answer.

I would have wallowed in this addictive wave of self-pity had it not been for my parents.

Thankfully, they didn't give up on me even though I had. They treated me just like a normal child and as a part of their unique and democratic parenting, my sister and I were enrolled for lawn tennis.

We were both put through the same rigour initially, but our coach soon threw up his hands. 'Your younger daughter is too weak for sports. She does not have enough stamina for lawn tennis,' he declared to my father.

My father, a history professor at DAV College, Amritsar, is a sports lover. Back in his days he was a state-level lawn tennis player. We grew up watching him play. He wanted to pass on his love for lawn tennis to his children as an inheritance.

So when my father heard the coach, he was furious; he did not take the comment from the coach lightly. 'I will train you girls myself and don't you ever call my child weak or sick,' he shouted at the coach.

He started coaching me and my sister and ensured that I did not get any special treatment under his tutelage. Yes, I had to do the same workouts as my sister. We used to wake up early in the morning and train for a couple of hours before school. Then when Papa came from college in the evening we were already there in the tennis courts for evening practice. He never allowed me to rest even when I got breathless. 'How cruel he is!' shrieked people who watched him train me. But we both knew why he was doing it. Our dear father never really cared about what the world had to say. His only words to us were:

Mat kar tu reham itna, ki dusra ise teri kamzori samajh le,
Mat kar tu pyar itna, ki koi tere dil ko khilona samajh khel jaye,
Bas kar tu karam apna, ki mehnat ka fal tera adhikar ban jaye.
(Do not show so much compassion, that others take it as your weakness,
Do not love so much, that anyone will toy your heart and break it,
Just keep doing your karma, the fruit of hard work will become your right.)

Lawn tennis changed everything for me. For the first time in my life I was out in the open, playing in the sun without any worries, just like a normal kid. I wasn't exceptional at the game but I was happy to just play. It was more about having fun than competing. Playing the game was never about winning. Lawn tennis was my release.

When others would fight, crib, cry and be happy about losing or winning a point or a game, I was the odd one out as I was always happy even when I lost. For me to be able to play like the rest was more important than winning. But my father realized I was getting complacent and he was not going to let me get away with it. He started training me harder and longer. I soon figured out that even though I was treated differently by my schoolmates, when I played lawn tennis, I was treated as an equal. I was a player, not a dadima or defective piece. I had something to look forward to in life. I was still not really in it to win it. I simply loved the idea of engaging in a sport that made me feel good about myself. But after I got my first taste of bitter defeat at my first tournament, it occurred to me that I could never accept myself as a loser.

Gradually, my game improved. I became addicted to winning and it made me popular in school and social circles. The winning streak boosted my confidence so much that I began to take part in other cultural activities as well. The quiet, reticent, weak girl was gone; instead I was out in the sunshine—active, social and popular. In fact, I was now a small-town sports celebrity along with my sister and brother, with whom I was unbeatable in doubles. I began dreaming of a career in sports.

But a career in sports in this country is fraught with too many challenges. In a family where all three kids had similar aspirations, pursuing lawn tennis at a professional level was out of the question, unless I was exceptional. When I started taking stock, I realized that I was nowhere close to being in the top rung to expect my family to invest all their resources in my fantasy. And I could not even blame anyone for it.

With my aspirations thwarted, I became rebellious again and wanted to escape from Amritsar. I was sure once I got out of there, I would be able to get things done my way. I began by enrolling in a management programme in Bengaluru.

I was naïve enough to believe that once I was on my own, I could control my life, my destiny.

Little did I know that my best laid plans were about to go awry.

2

Losing My Soul, Finding My Love

SPORTS AND EXTRACURRICULAR activities have no use in the corporate world, which was all about your designation and your salary. This is what I learned in Bengaluru, where I landed up when I was barely nineteen years old. I wanted to start afresh and thanks to all the glorified images of a successful corporate career, I thought a degree in management studies was my big ticket to the good life and respect in society.

But on my own, without my family to fall back on, I was faced with the harsh reality of my chosen profession. It was nothing like what they feed us on TV and in books. The first lesson I learned was that sports and extracurricular activities had no use in the corporate world. It was all about the brand you worked with, your designation and your salary. This was the reality and it was thrust on to me without any sugar coating. I was alone and had no family to soften the blow. I even started questioning about my youth and spent all my time in playing and taking part in extracurricular activities. Was it all a waste? The two years of management study changed me as a person. I was now living by myself, in a rented apartment and facing the world alone, with my head held high

I was twenty-one-and a half when I got a job with an MNC. I was 'set for life'.

Unfortunately for me, that life was now all about targets, month-ends, incentives and promotions.

My family took a back seat. In the few minutes of hurried telephonic conversations with them back home, I heard them speak about their lives, but nothing registered, nothing interested me. My life, my work, my foreign trips were more exciting.

I hardly used to visit my parents. Neither did I encourage them to come to Bengaluru. In fact, my father and sister never visited me in those years. It was only my mom who came down to be with me whenever I was sick. And that would happen maybe once or twice a year. She kept her visits short, and I did not hold her back. So engrossed was I with my work life that I did not really care about celebrating family milestones with them anymore. I missed my parents' twenty-fifth wedding anniversary as it coincided with the month-end procedures and I didn't want to jeopardize my target. I missed my sister's wedding functions as I was travelling abroad on top performers' forums at the Asia level, which was important for me to get noticed by my seniors. Worse, I started judging people on the basis of their grades and salary.

I had lost my soul. And I was about to give up on my body too.

Bengaluru is nicknamed the 'garden city' of India. It has pleasant weather and plenty of greenery but it is not kind to people suffering from asthma thanks to the high density of pollen in the air. Coupled with the explosion in the construction industry, the city played havoc on my health.

Despite knowing that nature is not kind to me, I picked up the fad of being skinny.

Instead of adopting a healthy lifestyle, I took the easy way out. I had given up lawn tennis due to crazy work hours but I even stopped indulging in any kind of physical activity that could make me hungry. My new diet plan involved skipping meals, lots of caffeine, junk food, coffee and corn—just enough to keep hunger at bay. I weighed less than 45 kg and I was proud of it. And added to it all was my work pressure. There were so many times that I had to be rushed to hospital, sometimes because of asthma attacks and sometimes due to weakness. The reason was obvious—an unhealthy lifestyle. My mother and doctors tried hard to bring me back on track but I was high on success and getting into size 0 dresses and did not give a damn.

I lost a lot of things during the time I spent in Bengaluru, but I gained a lot as well—it was in Bengaluru that Arvind, my husband, came into my life.

Arvind was my colleague and we had several common interests. As we began spending more and more time together, he noticed what a poor eater I was. Arvind was a foodie and he gradually started ensuring that I ate properly whenever we went out for lunch or dinner.

I started with soup and salads and thanks to his monitoring and encouragement, I graduated to main courses. My health improved even though I started getting critical about my weight.

Arvind was a positive influence on my life in more ways than one. He made me realize that I was making a huge mistake by being cold and indifferent to my family and that I had some dues to pay.

So when I got an offer from my company to relocate to Chandigarh, close to my family, he encouraged me to take it up. I was not very keen to take up the job, even though it had a higher profile. Not only was Bengaluru a much more cosmopolitan city, I was also feeling awkward about reconnecting with my family, who would now be much closer to me once I moved to Chandigarh. I loved my independence and carefree life in Bengaluru. I knew getting closer to home would mean more involvement of my family in my life and I would have to change many things. I was not ready for any change.

But I did eventually give in and moved to Chandigarh. My entire family came from Amritsar to Chandigarh to welcome me. My newly wed sister came with her husband. The first thing that hit me was that everyone I had willingly left behind seemed to be the same. After ignoring my sister for more than four years, I was now back in her life, and as though no time had passed, she was there for me, rock-solid, just like when we were young. Nothing had changed, other than the fact that she was married. To add to my guilt, she happily took charge of my life when I had my asthma attacks, rebuked me, consoled me, fussed over me and made me feel better by simply hearing me out after a bad day at work... I just kept asking myself, why and how did I become the person that I was?

Back in the midst of all that I had once held dear but of late, had ignored, I began to value relationships. I made it a point to visit my parents every weekend and spend ample time with them to make up for those lost days. I started turning down all foreign trips.

I took a long, hard look at myself and realized that I needed to get back in shape and that, too, in a healthy way. I started practising yoga and began going for evening walks around the beautiful Sukhna Lake. I also squeezed in a round of lawn tennis every once in a while with my sister in Chandigarh or whenever I was in Amritsar. After a long time, I was living a healthier life.

After I took up yet another job offer in Delhi, I had more time to focus on myself. And of course, on Arvind. During my stint in Chandigarh, he had been transferred to Delhi. We met more often, and spoke more often too. He turned out to be a great listener and every time I had to unburden myself, or simply rant about my family or work, I found it easy and comforting to confide in him. And after dating for a while,

I introduced Arvind to my parents. By the end of 2009, we were married.

I was hopeful about my life with Arvind; he knew everything about my past and my health. He knew that I was an asthma patient and had attacks during the season change when excess pollution and pollen affected me. But he had no idea what he was getting into until we got married.

Our wedding was in late October and by the time we were back from our holiday, it was the onset of winter.

I started getting asthma attacks and most of our nights were spent awake—when it was worst we were in some emergency room, where I would be administered a nebulizer. During every nebulization I would pass out. I would wake up an hour later to see my husband waiting by the bed to take me home.

The stress and frustration started creeping into our daily lives and we started getting irritated—with each other as well as others around. This was not the honeymoon period I had dreamed of.

As winter turned colder, my condition deteriorated. We bought a nebulization kit that I would be able to use on my own at home, but it still meant sleepless nights for both of us. In time my body adjusted to winter and the attacks became fewer. But I knew at the back of my mind that in a couple of months the weather would change and so would my life. I didn't want to go through that again. I could now relate to why kids called me 'defective piece' and 'dadima'. It was now time to fight back.

I started reading up on asthma and spoke to various doctors on how best I could keep the attacks at bay. I knew the secret—exercise.

Delhi has some of the best sports facilities in India that are open to the public. But it is not the most women-friendly city, especially late in the evenings. So while Delhi gave me access to lawn tennis or other sports, it turned out to be impractical after office hours.

Fortunately, we were staying in a part of south Delhi known for its gated colonies, police supervision and small parks with running tracks. We had a park just outside our house with a 400-m walking track. I didn't have much of an idea about running as an exercise or as a sport. The only running I had done was for warming up before playing lawn tennis.

My mornings were all about getting ready for office, leaving me with no time to exercise. I used to be home early, and rather than wait for my husband to get back from work, I used to walk down to the park where I saw people of all ages jogging. I could see them huffing and panting but never stopping. They all seemed unusually happy and content even after the strain they had put their body through. I was intrigued and wanted to try it out.

So one fine day, I put on my tennis shoes, grabbed my iPod and started to run. Halfway through the first lap I was gasping for air and felt as if my chest would explode. I stopped and walked the remaining stretch.

It was a wake-up call.

I was slim but also very weak. And I hated being weak. The nightmares of my childhood were coming back. My lifestyle of no exercise had killed my stamina.

But rather than get frustrated I took this up as a challenge. Being a tennis player, I had top-notch sports gear and I was back on the track the next day with a vengeance. I wasn't going to let the distance defeat me, though at first, it was very tough not to give up. My body screamed for me to quit but I just ignored it and pushed myself to continue. Unlike most runners who track their progress gradually, I was not bothered about any such thing. I wanted to add a lap every day. The first couple of days were difficult and it was tougher to add a lap every day. Some days I managed to keep pushing myself but there were also days when I couldn't. I persisted never stopping till my body simply refused to take another step. My perseverance paid off and soon I was able to do ten laps without a break.

As I started to push myself further and further, my legs and feet began to hurt. I tried to ignore the aches and pains, hoping that they would heal on their own. But as I started running longer distances, the pain became difficult to ignore.

I mentioned this to my husband and we arrived at the conclusion that I had made the most basic mistake of a novice runner—I was running without the correct shoes. The very next day I bought my first pair of running shoes. I still have them with me.

The first day I ran in my new shoes I felt like I was flying and ended up completing twelve laps. I was delighted. My running improved as well. I didn't feel any pain and was able to run longer.

I also started modifying my iPod playlist to listen to more adrenaline-pumping songs—'Ride it' by Jay Sean was my favourite. Peppy music made me forget the distance and made the run more enjoyable as well. In four months I was doing twenty laps daily on an average.

Winter was fast approaching. It came as a pleasant surprise when I didn't have a single asthma attack during the time the weather turned. Running was clearly helping me fight asthma. But I was still a bit sceptical. I focused on running and was now averaging about twenty-five laps a day. Each day that I was away from the hospital, I grew more confident.

Running became my religion.

I was contented and finally settled in Delhi. My job was fun and my personal life was rocking. I was not a weakling anymore. Most importantly, I was ready to have a baby.

But just when I thought things were finally settling down, life shook up my precious apple cart again. Arvind got transferred to Mumbai in October 2011 and now I had to move to Mumbai with him. The plan of starting a family took a back seat and we were now busy relocating and getting myself transferred to Mumbai in the same job.

3

A City on the Run

UNLIKE MILLIONS WHO follow their dreams to Mumbai, I reached the city with nothing but resentment in my heart for having to give up my beautiful life in Delhi. It did not help that from the moment we landed, nothing seemed to be going our way. The landlord who had accepted a token amount from us for letting out his apartment, ditched us at the last moment and we were forced to shift into the guesthouse provided by Arvind's company while we waited for our furniture to arrive from Delhi.

The days were hectic, and I had no time to run. We spent weeks hunting for a house, juggling our jobs. We wanted a place in west Khar or Bandra, because it would be closer to our offices and I could run in the neighbourhood parks that were considered safe even in the evenings.

After around forty-five days and endless search, we found a place that was more viable than we could expect. It turned out to be the first and biggest turning point for us in Mumbai.

After the initial busy days of moving in, Arvind and I went back to focusing on our work. My old routine was back; in the morning I made breakfast, got ready for work, did some household chores; then after the long day at work, I would come home, cook and serve dinner and after that go for my daily run. Running and I once again united.

In Delhi I was the only woman I knew who ran late in the evenings. But on Carter Road, Mumbai, running seemed to be a way of life. I saw many strong runners, both men and women. The best part was that it didn't matter if the roads were narrow, had potholes or were congested with traffic—people were running and motorists were making way for them. Wow! I couldn't believe my eyes. I was happy with my decision to move to Khar. Finally, after weeks of sulking, I was my old self again. And it made Arvind happy to see I was feeling better about myself. In the evenings, we began talking again, and not just about work and mundane things—we had other stories to share. We were in love again.

That's when my husband—who had also noticed the passion and seriousness of the runners—told me about the upcoming Standard Chartered Mumbai Marathon to be held in 2011 on 16 January.

'Maybe that's why we see so many people running in groups every morning. You should give it a shot too,' he suggested.

The next day, I woke up early and went for the morning run to Joggers' Park. It was tough as I was no more used to morning run since I used to run at night after 9 p.m. However, I managed to run my target distance. After finishing my laps, I struck up a conversation with a bunch of runners who were stretching next to me. One of them suggested that I register for the half-marathon and gave me the details of the registration process.

Those days I often wondered how quickly life was reshuffling my priorities, like a pack of cards. There I was in Delhi just the other day, planning to visit my family in Amritsar for Lohri. And now I was focused on signing up for the half-marathon. I had missed the last date for the registration, but I was not willing to give up. At the suggestion of my Carter Road co-runners, a day before the marathon I reached the exposition where runners had gathered to pick up their allocated bibs.

The venue was buzzing. There were runners of all ages, shapes and sizes. There were physically challenged people as well as senior citizens. It was inspiring and humbling. 'I just *have* to be a part of this,' I told myself.

After some persistent effort, I finally managed to meet the event managers and requested them to register me. They said they had bibs only for the full marathon. I immediately said yes. I wanted to run, and they were giving me an opportunity. That's all that mattered.

While the event manager was waiting for the payment, I was still confused about whether I should take this full marathon bib or not. 'Can I make a call? I need to call my husband to inform him,' I told the manager. The manager nodded and tried to take the bib from my hand, but I hung on to it. With the bib in my hand, I called up Arvind.

'Arvind, I'm at the Mumbai Marathon expo. They say I can register but only for 42 km, not 21 km. I'm confused... should I take it?'

My darling husband did not take any time to reply. 'There's nothing to be confused about. Go for 42. I know you can do it easily. Just register.'

'Love you!'

The event manager was looking at me, waiting for my decision. I smiled and said, 'How much?'

4

My First Marathon

'HAVE YOU LOST it? Withdraw your name at once! We are not allowing you to run. What if you faint and injure yourself? Who gave you this stupid idea?'

My mother's reaction was predictable, but not acceptable to me.

'Mama, if you cannot encourage me, don't discourage me either,' I retorted and hung up.

I was surprised and disappointed that my parents did not share my excitement about my first marathon. Weren't they the ones who encouraged me to take up sports? But I knew where it was coming from.

My mother, who herself is head of radiology in Government Medical College, Amritsar, is the strongest person in our family. She is the one who holds our family together. She is our 'Iron Woman'. When we were growing up, she used to preach to us, 'Remember, kids, that to raise the bar you have to challenge the limits.' Sometimes I would tell her, 'Mama, people say I should not play tennis. Sports is not meant for me.' She would snap, looking into my eyes, 'When the world says "no" it means a "yes".'

But things changed after I fell sick just after my wedding. When my parents visited me in Delhi at the time, I was sick and still striking a balance between work and my personal life. Seeing this they got worried. Since then my mom and my older sister started calling me every day, twice a day, to keep a check on me.

Even though now I was doing fine and was healthy my parents were no more carefree when it came to me.

I decided not to talk to anyone else at home regarding the marathon as Mama would have already broken the news—they would be worried and have sleepless nights thinking about me. I did not want any tension and confusion. Besides, Arvind assured me that he would handle my parents and that I should just relax. Nonetheless, I wanted to share my enthusiasm with my runner friends, who had encouraged me to participate in the marathon. I hoped they would share some survival tips with me. But to my disappointment, they turned out to be less encouraging, the proverbial wet blankets. 'Sumedha, you are not prepared for 42 km. You should withdraw. You have never even run 21 km, how will you run 42 km? Running in a park is different from running a marathon,' they declared, hoping to dissuade me. But their voices did not reach my ears, filled as they were with the sound of my heart thumping with excitement.

On the day of the marathon, I woke up with a start as all the alarms that I'd set went off simultaneously. The bed was too inviting, but I fought against the urge to crawl back into it and got ready. My favourite shoes—check; my iPod with my favourite songs—check; my favourite running gear—check. I was ready for my first marathon. Arvind was with me, even though he is not a morning person.

I was constantly in touch with the other runners, who were already at the venue. I hopped into a local train—the fastest means to travel in Mumbai—and reached the venue on the dot. The race had started. The start flag had flagged off. I didn't have any time to warm up or stretch, but it's not like I was very diligent about it even though I know it's important; I was a self-taught, self-styled running enthusiast. I scrambled to join the great mass of people at the starting line; my first marathon had begun.

The first thing I noticed was how inadequate my running gear was. People were carrying water bottles, diet supplements, headlights. I didn't quite understand the need for these accessories but soon it hit me how woefully ill-equipped I was to run such a long distance. Had I bitten off more than I could chew?

Hoping to find my rhythm, I put on my favourite music. I had no idea of how much distance I had covered or for how long I had been running, but I simply kept following the pack and hoped for the best.

One of my biggest mistakes during my practice sessions was not drinking any water during the run. I used to drink water after the run was done and sometimes after I got home. That old habit came back to bite me now, just as it would bite me many months later at a very crucial time.

I was nearing the halfway point. On the way, I had seen several water stations offering fluids and people carrying water packs. I had stopped only once for a few gulps of water and wondered what the need was for so many water stops; I was about to find out. We were about to cross the iconic sea link.

The sun was beating down mercilessly and an 8-km stretch of heated tar lay before us. With the bright sun, no shade and few water stations, running became tougher. I ran briskly for about 5 km and then, a raging thirst hit me.

I was so dehydrated, I couldn't run anymore. I started to drag my feet, which had begun to feel heavier with each passing minute. One of the expert runners realized my predicament and offered me water. Grateful and rejuvenated, I completed the killer stretch and stopped at the first water station.

There, I made another mistake. I drank too much water too fast. I felt bloated and couldn't run. And I still had another 12 km to go.

For the first time ever, I began to think of quitting. I was very disappointed and angry with myself. Suddenly, I heard a voice: 'Let's run together and finish this damn thing.' I saw another runner, older than me, exhausted, but with his heart set on finishing the marathon.

He inspired me and I began to keep pace with him. We chatted intermittently. His name was Anand Venkatraman and it was his first full marathon too. He wouldn't believe that this was my first-ever run and was shocked when I told him that I had not been drinking water while running.

We decided to finish under five hours. And we managed to push ahead to reach the end comfortably. His parting words were: 'Buy a watch for the next run.'

But the big surprise of the day was—I completed fifteenth in the open women's category.

I called up my parents. Arvind told me they had been calling him every few minutes to check on me. 'I proved you wrong!' I almost yelled into the phone in excitement.

'Thank you! I knew it,' said my mom. I could hear the heaviness in her voice. It was just like my tennis days.

That day changed me. My parents became more confident about me; they didn't worry about my health anymore. I became part of the marathon community and also learned my first crucial lessons in running—keep yourself hydrated and keep taking small bites like nuts, or from bananas or a protein bar when low on energy during the run. With that also came the right gear, the right accessories—and the desire to keep running.

Suddenly, life was baiting me with more opportunities.

After a few months, Arvind and I were to go to Malaysia, to visit my in laws. My father-in-law and mother-in-law who were also proud of my achievement in the recent marathon, told me about a marathon there and I promptly enrolled. This time, I felt better prepared and wanted to improve my timing. But when I ran, walked and finally crawled to the finishing line, I realized I hadn't done my homework. Proximity to the equator and the consequent heat changed everything. Even then, I had come in sixth, which was a huge confidence-booster.

High on running, I wanted to get into ultra-marathons now. There was one coming up in Bengaluru. There were three options—100 km, 75 km and 50 km. I wanted to do the 100 km. But when I asked a veteran who had already done the 100-km run, he threw a spanner in the works. 'Sumedha, you are not trained enough for the ultra-marathon. Besides,' he said, 'your timings are good for marathons. If you want to run for anything beyond 50 km, you should start training this year and only give it a shot next year.'

Arvind, my staunchest ally, also thought I was being unrealistic and I decided to stop discussing the matter with anyone for a while. I was sore and irritated at the obvious lack of faith in my abilities.

The next day, Arvind and I went for a stroll and ran into the same runner who had discouraged me earlier. Once again he insisted that I should not do anything more than 50 km. It was only then that Arvind perhaps sensed my frustration. I asked my husband again, 'Can I run 100 km?'

'Run 75,' he said with a twinkle in his eye. I looked at him and kissed him, and without another word, signed up for the marathon. Later that night I could not help but ask him: 'Baby, why 75 km and not 100?'

Arvind smiled and said, 'See, 75km sounds achievable. Run 75 km and see how you fare in it. Let 100 km be your next goal. But you better tell your parents about your decision.'

Soch gambhir ho to faisle kamzor ho jaate hain

(Deep thoughts can weaken decisions.)

I was now going to run my first ultra-marathon and my third running event for the calendar year. I was happy.

I wanted to stall yet another confrontation with my family till we met in Amritsar for Diwali.

5

Press Pause for Motherhood

DIWALI ARRIVED AND we were on our way to Amritsar to meet my parents.

It was the first break for me in a long phase of reading, preparing and training myself.

It was difficult for me to take a break from practice, as the run was only a few days away. I was running wherever I could—the treadmill at the gym, on running tracks and lawn tennis courts. I was practising six days a week. My family could not understand this sudden interest in running that I had picked up. I was apprehensive about breaking the news to them. But there were a lot of awkward questions being asked and I decided to come clean once and for all.

I still remember that night. The family was still in the puja room performing the Diwali rituals. After the ceremony, my grandparents were distributing prasad, when my grandmother said to me, 'Chinu, next time you visit us, you must come with our grandchild. We are old and want to see your baby soon!'

I remained quiet. Everyone in the room was looking at me expectantly.

I mustered the courage to speak up at last, 'Amma, ask Arvind. After all, it's his decision too.'

Despite my efforts to shift the focus to my husband, my family members, who know me only too well, began counselling me. Almost all of them started to speak at once until I could not take it any longer.

I blurted out, 'But I don't want to be a mother yet!'

There was a stunned silence in the room, punctured only by the noise of the crackers outside.

It was my mother who spoke up first, 'Is this any way to speak?'

'I want to run 75 km in Bengaluru this November, and I have registered for it already. I want your blessings,' I said, trying to sound as composed as possible.

My grandparents turned to Arvind, 'What is that?'

My brother came to our rescue, and explained to them in hushed whispers what I was talking about.

Arvind somehow was not happy with my reply. He knew I was nervous but he was not aware of what was going in my mind. He didn't like the way I was throwing the blame on him for delaying whereas the truth was the opposite. 'Sumedha wants to focus on running right now and we will plan a baby next year,' he said politely.

I nodded quietly, tears streaming down my cheeks. A year back, I wanted to have a baby and I was planning for it. Now I could not even bear to think about it.

I gulped down my tears and said, 'I knew you would disapprove of my running the marathon. I know you think like so many people around the world that running ruins the knees. But I have found my passion. I am addicted to it and there is no cure.'

The puja room was eerily quiet when I finished. Had I ruined Diwali for everyone? My father came to me, hugged me and wiped my tears.

'We all want you to be happy,' he said tenderly. 'We have seen you in so much pain when you were a kid that we don't want you to suffer again. Please don't ever hate us...we are parents and it hurts us to see our children getting hurt. You will always remain a child for us. Having a kid is a matter of choice. Please plan it when you want it. We are with you. Have you registered for the marathon?'

I nodded my head.

Papa turned to Arvind. 'Please take care of her and make sure she trains well.'

'Thank you, Papa,' I smiled at him and apologized to my mother. She hugged me, kissed me and said, 'Don't hate me just because I object to your plans. I'm your mother. I love you more than my life.'

The next day, we were to fly back from Delhi. My parents

came to see us off at the Amritsar railway station. I was under a heavy load of guilt—I hated the fact that I was turning out to be the perfect problem child who made her family go through this emotional crisis. It was not a pleasant goodbye, but a tearful one as I held on to my parents, even while they insisted that I always listen to my heart.

The night before my flight to Bengaluru, my father called to wish me luck. He also asked me to check my email.

Dear Chinu,

Everyone aspires to achieve success but looks for a magic wand, well knowing its basic ingredients are perspiration, persistence and determination. Most give up early and feel contented with material fulfilment and end up cursing destiny or playing the blame game. But few continue to strive and try, defying fate and accomplishing the feat. Triumph comes to determined deeds.
Best of luck.

Love,
Papa

We reached Bengaluru a day before the run. It had been three years since I had left the city where I got my first job, met Arvind and above all, created an identity for myself. Today I was back to create yet another identity for myself—that of an ultra-marathoner.

The day of the marathon finally dawned. We reached the

venue and I took my place at the starting line.

As I was self-trained, I used to make my own training plans, which could fit my routine life. Most of the training plans available on the internet were sixteen weeks long and they were not meant for me. I started reading tips for running ultra-marathons and any other articles related to it and tried to incorporate them during my training. I started wearing a water belt while running, munching nuts while running and doing specific stretches before and after a run.

I had trained well for this event but I was completely blank when I reached the starting line. I had no clarity about how I would run, was not too sure about how to pace myself or how much I could stretch myself. In the end I came up with a simple solution. Run for 42 km, since I had already done that, and walk the remaining stretch, making sure I finish without getting myself injured. I had nothing to lose anyway. Moreover, for the first time, I was completely prepared—I was carrying my iPod, a GPS sports Garmin watch, a water bottle, a headlamp and chocolate bars.

The Bengaluru ultra-team had devised a new route for that year's run. It was narrow and undulating and we had to do multiple loops. Early morning, when the 100-km and 75-km marathons were flagged off, the number of runners was fewer in this than the other categories.

I was able to run well. The cool Bengaluru weather helped me cover a considerable distance early, before the crowd of the remaining categories joined us.

Once the other runners came on board, doing a 16-km loop became even more difficult. But my headstart helped. Soon I crossed the 40-km mark and started walking.

Another couple of hours later, I found myself advancing at a good speed and my body was adapting well to the conditions. I felt brave enough to try running and I was able to make good time. I continued to take care of my hydration and suddenly, there was only one loop left. I tried not to hurry up in my excitement, lest I get injured, but maintained a steady pace—and finished as the winner in my category!

I never considered myself to be a great runner. But running the ultra-marathon made me realize that it is more about mental strength than anything else. I loved the high. I loved the challenge.

Long-distance running is not just about training, stamina or talent. It has more to do with controlling your mind and building your perseverance.

I had found my calling. My plans were made—the Mumbai Marathon in January 2012 and the Comrades in June 2012. Comrades is the world's oldest and largest ultra-runs held in South Africa, and I had set my heart on it.

But when has life ever followed a script?

Back in Mumbai I began training diligently for the Comrades run. I began to practise on slopes and worked on my speed and I could see the results. My running seemed to improve tremendously. The Comrades medal seemed to be within my reach—at least till that fateful day.

9 December 2011. It was a month before the Mumbai Marathon. I was practising at night, when out of the blue, a car hit me and sped away.

6

Reading the Signs

FOR A MOMENT, I thought I had lost my limbs.

With the help of people around me, I managed to get up on my feet and take a few tentative steps. The wounds on my knees did not bother me, but as long as my limbs were not broken, I was thankful. Instead of going home straightaway, I walked the remaining stretch. It was painful but I wanted to do it, just to ensure that my limbs were intact.

Later, we consulted an orthopaedist, who pronounced that along with the few sprains in my body, I had a low vitamin D and vitamin B_{12} count. It was also diagnosed that I was suffering from lumbar spondylitis, the degenerative bone disease, which was compressing the nerve and leading to pain in my left leg; and the accident just brought it out in the open.

I was crushed. I was just twenty-eight years old. I was

already asthmatic, hadn't yet had any children and now I had one more health issue to tackle.

Was I to blame for my condition? That was the question on my mind.

But all I could ask the doctor was, 'Can I ever run again?'

The doctor gave me a little reassuring smile: 'Of course! Why do you think you will not be able to? You just cannot run now, because it will worsen your condition. Take a three-month break. With physiotherapy and medication you will be all set to run again.'

Arvind was not entirely convinced. He enquired, 'Is there anything to worry about?'

'Not at all,' the doctor assured us again.

Taking the doctor's advice to heart, I gave up running; I only walked. But with the marathon approaching, I was itching to, even though my injury had not healed completely. Everyone around me was only talking about the Mumbai Marathon, making it a very frustrating period for me. Despite all the warnings, and the pain, I decided to push myself a bit and began to run again.

I called the event manager of the marathon who was aware of my condition. He was surprised when I told him I wanted to run again. 'Why don't you run the half marathon?' he suggested when I went to meet him.

'I cannot afford to miss the full marathon,' I told him bluntly. 'I need the timing on record to qualify for the Comrades.'

I had to submit my certificate by 1 May 2012. I begged and pleaded with him, and knowing my headstrong nature, he eventually—though very reluctantly—signed me on.

Overjoyed with the bib in my hand, I got back into the car. Arvind was quiet. He did not even look at me but kept staring straight ahead, his hands gripping the steering wheel. There seemed to be a storm raging in his mind.

'What has happened to you?' he began slowly, taking a lot of effort to utter the words.

'Baby, when you started, you were running for fun, for the sheer joy of it. Now it is all about some damn event to win, some milestone to achieve. You get stressed out when you are not able to run well or your timings are not good. What's going on?'

I was stung. But Arvind did not stop.

'I don't think you should run. You need to heal yourself. Bone ageing is not an injury. It is an internal weakness. You are running this marathon for your ego and nothing else. What are you trying to prove? That you are stronger than what people think? If you are really strong, your ego will not defeat you. This run is all about your ego and you will get nothing other than more pain...an aching body and an aching soul—that's all that you will be left with.'

I looked outside the car. There were joyful runners with their bibs. I looked at Arvind but I didn't say a word. I wanted to finish with strong timings to my credit and to prove everyone wrong. Yes, I did want to do this for my ego.

Mumbai Marathon 2012. The day had started with all the wrong signs.

The night before the marathon, I developed a nagging pain in my ankle because of incorrect stretching and it was worse in the morning. Painkillers and sprays were not helping either. I called up a fellow runner, to seek his advice. He said, 'You must run, Sumedha, simply because you love running. Abandon the race at any point your body gives up.'

Arvind overheard our conversation and was evidently unhappy with the way things were turning out. 'I don't think you should go for the marathon. You are not in any condition to run,' he said with an arm around my shoulders. His words did not even reach me. Comrades was well within my reach. I just knew it. And I chose to ignore anything that would contradict my conviction. All the signs that countered my belief were ignored.

This time, once again, I reached late for the marathon. With just three minutes to flag off, the event management team was kind enough to allow me to enter.

I started well and soon found my rhythm. I was aiming at a four-hour finish. My ego boosted me towards a strong run for the first 18 km. And then my legs began to fail me.

Refusing to acknowledge the warning signs, I walked for 100 metres and then started running again. But this time I realized I was limping more than running. My mind kept tricking me into believing that I was still in good shape. My watch did a perfect job of recording my timing, but said nothing of my emotions. I could not keep lying to myself. The thought of improving my timing made my legs feel heavier by the second. I was dragging myself ahead, but my ego was still not allowing me to listen to my body. I had covered just 20 km and still 22 km were to go but my mind finally gave in. Along with swollen ankle, I had, shooting pain down my left leg and I couldn't lift my leg anymore. I didn't call for medical help. I didn't want the world to know I was injured and that I was weak. I simply called Arvind.

'I'm calling it off,' I said, and walked away from the route.

He sounded concerned. 'Where are you?'

'I'm at sea link flyover near Lilavati,' I was choking on my emotions, gasping for air. 'I don't want to go home right now. I want to clear my mind. I'll see you at Bandstand.'

My husband had only one thing to say, 'Baby, you took a brave decision.' I could sense the relief in his voice. He was waiting for me at the finishing line near VT station, which I could not reach. 'I'm glad you're thinking about your health first I respect you even more now; you wait for me at Bandstand and I will catch the train to Bandra. Wait for me,' he said. I agreed and said, 'Arvind, I'm sorry' and disconnected the phone

I walked backwards, threw away the chip tied to my shoe and began to weep. I was in physical pain but my heart ached much more. In my mind I was all set to be the running star and I saw that star falling. I cried and cried. I sat at Bandstand and kept looking at the sea, thinking about what just happened. I struggled to hold back the tears, but they just wouldn't stop.

I had been tagged—DNF. Did Not Finish. Today, my ego had been completely defeated.

I had started the year on a disastrous note. It was my first marathon of 2012 and I could not finish it. I had also lost out on my chance at running the Comrades. No ointment could heal this wound.

I remembered the day when I walked into the court for my first-ever lawn tennis match. As kids, my brother and I used to play there often. It was special for my parents because it would be the first time that all their three children were playing in the same tournament.

I had cheered my sister when she won her matches there. I wanted her to do the same for me. My brother had already played and won his game. I was confident I could do the same.

My opponent was a novice, and someone with whom I had often practised. I was excited at the prospect of beating her. *It would be too easy,* I thought. *I will be hailed as the next big thing in lawn tennis and everyone would want to play with me and try to defeat me.*

With such delusions of grandeur I stepped into the court, started playing and even won my first two games when anxiety got the better of me.

Then, I began to make mistakes. My sister and brother, who were there with my parents, were constantly cheering for me, egging me on. My sister, in fact, was the voice of wisdom. 'Don't be overconfident. Just relax,' she said, but I just could not get back to my game. I lost the game by 2-6 and I was out of the tournament. I was so ashamed that I began to bawl. Not only because I had lost, but I was defeated by one over whom I had triumphed easily so many times before.

That incident proved to be a turning point for me. I was just not prepared to lose anymore. I began to practise more seriously and kept reminding myself, 'It is not just about the joys of participating, but winning is as important.'

I thought of that day today, as I sat there on Bandstand, at the end of the race I had abandoned midway. It seemed to me as though I had given up without a fight. I was angry with myself and kept questioning my intent, or the lack of it. 'Why did I give up? So what if I finished with bad timing? Am I not a true sportsperson? How could I just give up?'

When Arvind arrived at Bandstand, I threw myself at him and wailed. 'Baby,' he said gently, as he looked at my swollen ankle and the agony writ large on my face. 'You would have got your certificate and earned some praise, but you would have lost your love for running forever. I am glad you listened to your body and stopped.'

I knew he was right. But my heart still ached at the thought of missing out on Comrades. Arvind read my mind. 'Listen,' he said, 'For Comrades we can try another run in April. You have three months to recover. All is not lost.'

I was a quitter. All that mattered to me was this thought. Despite Arvind exhorting me to plan for Comrades by giving my body the rest it deserved, I could not forget the fact that I had walked out of a race midway. But rather than wallow in self-pity, I was back researching on the international events where I could run to qualify for Comrades. I found one in Switzerland.

Running abroad takes a lot of investment—money, mind and body. I checked with my doctor first, who advised me to proceed cautiously. I began with hours of yoga and a couple of hours of walking. I drastically altered my diet, having 500 ml of curd every day to strengthen my bones, as well as bowls of pulses and black beans, combined with enough vitamins. The doctors finally gave me a clean chit.

On 26 February that year, I started running again. After two months of diligence, my mind and body were ready for Comrades. But the economy was not. And two marathons abroad suddenly were not a feasible idea anymore. I abandoned the idea of Switzerland and Comrades with a heavy heart. But someone, somewhere was planning a big surprise for me. Yet another life-altering experience was just around the corner, and I was blissfully unaware of it.

7

Dreaming Big

3 APRIL 2012: It was just another humdrum day at work until I got a call from Raj. I had first met Raj Vadgama at an amateur runners' meet.

I remember everyone talking about him reverentially as someone for whom a 100-km run was not a big deal. I was intrigued when he called me. Raj came straight to the point. He spoke to me about Greenathon.

'For the last three years we have been running to raise money and awareness for the environment,' he said. 'This year on 20 May, we plan to set a new record on Greenathon by running from New Delhi to Mumbai. That is, 1,500 km in thirty days. We want to build a team of four men and two competent women ultra-runners, which will be lead by Milind Soman. Would you like to join us?'

I did not want to think too much. My heart was pounding in my head. 'Yes, Raj, I'm ready to run this run,' I blurted out.

Raj asked 'What about your job?'

'I can handle my office but you will have to convince my husband,' I said excitedly.

'I'm not good at persuading. I can ask Milind to talk to him and to your office if need be,' he replied.

After a couple of anxious hours, I got a call from Milind. We were complete strangers introduced by Raj. He sounded surprisingly convinced about my endeavour and promised to talk to my husband.

But before that, I had to call up Arvind and tell him about the dramatic turn my life had taken in the past two hours.

There was a long silence after Arvind heard me out. And then he said, 'It's a big event and a big opportunity. We cannot make such a decision over the phone. We need to get all the facts in place before taking a call.'

'Milind will call you shortly,' I quipped. Arvind laughed. He knew me only too well.

That evening, Raj was the first to arrive at our place for the crucial meeting. He was a guy who ran with his heart, and it was obvious from the way he spoke of his experiences, his inspiration and his association with Milind. He also made it clear that despite the fact that I would have to forgo my month's salary for the run, we would not get paid. We were expected to do this for charity.

When Milind joined us, we were taken by surprise.

Dressed in a casual T-shirt and jeans, he looked nothing like the glamorous supermodel we all remembered him as.

Polite and professional, he asked me directly, 'So are you with us for the run from Delhi to Mumbai?'

'Why did you decide to run 1,500 km?' I asked him instead.

Milind replied, 'Well, last year everyone said 500 km in fifteen days was an impossible task. But we managed to finish that quite easily, and then we wanted to run some more. So we decided to raise the bar this time.' When I asked him about how everyone was training for the event, he shrugged and said, 'Frankly, I, or rather we, have no idea. We plan to learn and improvise as we go along.'

I didn't want to keep anyone in the dark about my injuries. After I told them about how I started running and what was holding me back, and my apprehensions about attempting something like this for the first time, Raj said, 'We all have our apprehensions about running such a long distance, without even knowing what to expect. Like I told you, we plan to build a team of six, including two women. The women will attempt to complete 750 km by running alternately, while the men will attempt to do the entire 1,500-km stretch. Remember, this is not a race, but an endurance run for a social cause. Completion is the main criteria. You need to clock 750 km in thirty days. That's all.'

Arvind, who had been quiet all this while, spoke up.

'Can you share details of the logistics, route and security for the women runners?' My heart skipped a beat. Was he actually saying yes?

Milind filled him in about the event—the organizers, the crew and the cars that would tag the runners to provide security and support on the road, and a doctor and a masseur who would be on call twenty-four hours. He also added that the women runners would be given special attention as the run would take the team across highways at odd hours.

'If she were to participate in the run would I be able to travel with you guys?' asked Arvind.

I wanted to jump up and kiss my husband.

'You are more than welcome to join us,' said Milind. But you will have to bear your own cost. Why do you want to do that? Don't you guys ever stay apart?'

I gave my husband a knowing smile. I get very cranky when he's not around and both of us try our best not to travel alone. I remembered the time when we shifted from Delhi to Mumbai; my husband had to travel ahead of me. For that one month, for every holiday and weekend when either one of us had to travel, turned out to be very stressful for us.

I realized what his mind was playing at; if he was not able to join me for the thirty days of the mega-run, at least on the holidays and weekends, there was a good chance that I would give up, pack my bags and run home. Call me a hopeless romantic, but when you are all alone in a city without your parents around, you become very dependent on each other.

My husband continued to ask pertinent, practical questions about the costs involved, and Milind patiently answered them all. I knew our biggest challenge was managing the financial resources which would come under considerable strain over this one month of my run. Especially since it was obvious that my husband would have to fly down to wherever I was over the weekends to be with me.

Milind did not make any promises about money but assured us that he would try and get a sponsor on board for our gear at least.

It was a start.

Now all eyes were back on my husband. He seemed to be lost in deep thought. He eventually looked up and addressed Milind and Raj, 'I would like to thank both of you for taking the time and effort to come home and discuss the details of the event with us. I do understand that for an event of this scale, people would be hounding you to be a part of it. But here you are, so graciously inviting my wife to join your team. From what you have just told me, the run will be well managed. The organizers are known to be very professional and I know I don't need to worry about the arrangements. They have been doing this for three years, haven't they? And that, too, successfully. However, I would like to share my apprehensions with you about my wife.'

Arvind paused. I gulped. Was he about to change his mind?

'You have probably picked the worst time for this run; it's the onset of summer,' continued Arvind. 'I do understand the dates cannot be changed but other than her recent slow recovery from an accident, she is also an asthma patient.

I am not sure how well she will cope with the dusty highways, especially during the harvest season. She is bound to have asthma attacks that will slow her down and require a lot more medical attention. I am worried about her going through thirty days in that condition.'

And then Arvind looked at me, his eyes betraying the tumult of emotion within. 'The problem with my wife is that she never gives up. So she will keep running till the time she's stopped by some external force, or if she has to be taken to a hospital. I am worried about her.'

At that moment, I fell in love with Arvind all over again. But I also wanted to make it clear that I was strong enough to do this. 'I have not had an asthma attack for at least a year now,' I piped in. 'I know you are worried about me. But I will take proper care and I promise not to have any health issues because of neglect. Besides, they have a doctor and I will also carry along a portable nebulization kit.'

Raj turned to Arvind, 'Don't worry, she is our responsibility. We will ensure that she is taken care of.' My husband nodded but wasn't completely convinced.

I wanted to immediately change the topic lest the green signals I noticed from my husband changed to red.

I said, 'I am slower than all of you. If ever I fall behind, will you guys ask me to leave?' The question had the desired effect and everyone in the room smiled and relaxed a bit. Milind said, 'We are a team. We don't leave anyone behind. And like I said before, you will always have a vehicle with you all the time.

This is not a race and we will complete the event as a team.'

The moment they left the house, I was literally sitting on my husband's head. 'Can I go? Can I go? Can I go?' I was doggedly pursuing him for an approval to follow my heart. The last time I was this desperate to get an approval was when I was waiting for my parent's nod to marry my husband. I guess excitement turns me into an irrational kid. But Arvind continued to play it down, much to my disappointment. 'This is a big decision and we both need to think about it,' he said. I tried to remain calm, but my mind was in turmoil. What if he said no?

I looked at my husband sleeping that night and felt extremely annoyed with him for leaving me hanging. I had no doubts about my own decision. I was ready to run. I also knew of my husband's apprehensions. I was a relatively new runner and probably not experienced enough for such a long haul. The timing of the run, the route as well as the running conditions would certainly aggravate my asthma condition and trigger frequent attacks. Besides, the travel and the upkeep would make a serious dent in our resources. I kept thinking about Arvind's concerns; they were mine too.

I must have dozed off in the wee hours of the morning when I was woken up by my husband. For a moment I thought all that had happened yesterday was a dream. But my husband quickly brought me back to reality with his opening remark, 'Baby, you must run and that, too, the entire 1,500 km. I know you can do it. I would not have asked you to do this if I had any doubts. Trust me.'

After my apprehension-filled phone calls to my family and their less-than-encouraging response, my father called me back in the afternoon. I seemed to have kicked up a storm in the family. They had spent hours discussing my decision between themselves. I was scared. But my father sounded more relaxed since our morning conversation. He wanted me to give him all the details of the event and he got that in the next half hour. He heard me out silently, asking me a few pertinent questions every now and then. Once I finished, he was quiet for a long time. I couldn't handle any rejection that day. He just asked me a question, 'I'm proud of you—I know that you like taking risks and you like to do things differently but still, why are you so adamant? Why do you want to participate in such a difficult event and take so many risks, especially after marriage? Have you thought about it ever? '

I was waiting all day to be given a chance to tell my side of the story. I opened up my soul to my father, 'Papa, this run will give me a chance to show the world how strong I have become. You remember the days when everyone said that I was too unfit to play lawn tennis and that I should stay indoors? Today I have been invited to be part of a team of runners that aims to set a new record in endurance running. That, too, as a woman. There are women who are much better runners than I am but someone believes I'm equally good. This is my redemption. This run is not just about records but for a cause. If with my sweat and hard work I can bring about even a small change in people, then it is worth it. Also, I want to break the myth that women are only meant to look good, get married and make babies. And I want to do that by running on the highways. I want you to stand with me and be proud of having a daughter like me; it is you who taught me how to be a fighter when I had given up as a child.'

My father replied, 'Go live your dreams. You are our child; our prayers and support are always with you. Prove to the world how wrong they are and make us all proud.' My eyes swelled with tears of joy.

Guru Govind dou khade, kaake lagoon paye, Balihari guru aapki, Govind diyo milaye.

(I face both God and my guru. Who should I bow to first? I first bow to my guru because he's the one who showed me the path to God.)

The thirty days of the run would eventually test my faith. The promises, the assurances and the trust would be tested and the scars would remain for a long time. But for now, I was in seventh heaven, looking forward to the opportunity of a lifetime.

8

The Twelve-day Plan

OUR AIRCRAFT WAS circling Delhi, when I peered through my window at the city spread out below with a sense of nostalgia. This is where I had started running. This is where I had started my married life. But now, I was touching down as a new person.

The twelve days leading up to the marathon had been packed. Now, instead of four men and two women, it was going to be five men and one woman. I was going to be the only woman participating in this run. I was now really worried as I thought another woman with me as a companion would have made the run easy.

Training and diet were the only priorities in my life.

I ran twice a day. In the sun, in the heat, and in the evenings. Sometimes I even ran back from the office. To acclimatize myself to the Indian roads, I even ate, slept and meditated on Carter Road. My diet was healthier now—I had 500 grams of homemade paneer, a lot of yogurt, peanuts, dates, spinach and fruits everyday. My water intake went up, as did my stamina. I also had Arvind constantly by my side when we went for walks, encouraging me all the time. I still wasn't fully confident, but my body was raring to go. To prepare my mind I began to read up on endurance running.

I learned the importance of walking in ultra-marathons and how many good runners ignore it at their own peril. I incorporated walking into my training, even though I hated it. I calculated that if an average ultra-runner, running at 9 km per hour, took a fifteen-minute break after three hours, I could catch up with him after four hours, provided I did not take that break.

I also consulted my orthopedist and underwent special massages to tone my body. I wanted to be 100 per cent fit and ready and was not willing to take any chances this time.

I was so engrossed in my training that I forgot that my sister's baby shower was coming up and that she was expecting my parents' first grandchild.

She had planned it around a time that would have been convenient for me to take a leave from work. Our tickets had been booked in February. I felt awful about missing this special day. But with the run just a week away, I was in a dilemma.

My sister, as always, understood me. 'Chinu, you have to practise hard. Now that you will be a *masi* soon, you better come back with stories of a lifetime for the little one. Don't you dare come back without completing the race...we will disown you.'

I hung up tearfully.

I often wondered at the way destiny always seemed to put me on an unconventional path. At a time when most married women of my age were busy having babies—after all it was the most logical thing to do in our country—I was busy training for my mammoth run.

The day before we left for Delhi, I met Raj and Milind at a Nike store where we were supposed to pick up our gear. That's where we were introduced to Apurba Dass, who had come with his family. Apurba's reputation as a strong runner preceded him.

Given his humble background, his passion for running and his infectious laughter, Arvind and I took to him immediately. The mood at the store was upbeat. I was dying to start running.

At home, after the last bit of careful packing for the days ahead when I would be on the road, I called up my parents. 'I can't embark on my journey without your blessings. They will be my only weapon in the days to come as I face the world and the challenge on my own. I need to hug you once before I start,' I told them.

My father was recovering from a serious operation and had been advised against travelling. But he had read my mind. 'If you can run for 1,500 km, I can travel 500 km. We have already booked our tickets to wish you luck. And we will also be there when you finish the run,' he announced. That was all I needed to hear.

My last night in Mumbai before I left on my epic adventure was emotional, poignant. I pottered around the house a bit, until my husband, sensing my anxiety, pulled me aside and kissed me. I could hardly sleep. I felt as though I would be leaving behind an important part of me.

We lay awake silently through the night in each other's arms. After two years of being married, we had finally discovered what it felt like to truly be in love.

I had dozed off on the flight to Delhi, but was wide-awake at touchdown. Milind was waiting at the guesthouse. This was the first time the entire team would be assembled together. We met the other runners, Mahesh Salvi and Sajjan Dabas, and collected the remaining gear.

This is how the team looked—Milind, Apurba and Raj were the 40s frontrunners, and Mahesh, Sajjan and I—the dark horse—were the young brigade.

Arvind left us all and went to work from one of his offices in Gurgaon and before I went off with my parents for some family time, I made sure I introduced them to my fellow runners. I was amused and touched at how my parents spoke to me as though I was still a child. But unlike a rebellious adolescent, I latched on to every word of advice, caution and inspiration they had for me.

'Don't stress yourself,' said my mother.

'Run with your brains, not just your legs. Walk if you

cannot run and crawl if you cannot walk. But finish the run and come home, else don't come,' said my father, my first coach, adding, 'I have a diary for you. You must write down your experiences. I want to see India through the eyes of a young woman.'

We were sitting outside a mall. I hugged my parents. 'I may not have been an ideal child, but you have been my idols and I will make you proud.'

We were supposed to start running at 4 a.m. from Qutub Minar the next morning. We needed to eat and sleep early. Arvind reached the guesthouse late. But we had a quick dinner and went to bed by 8.30 p.m. I slept like a baby in his arms that night; it seemed as though all my anxiety had melted away.

It was just me and the run ahead of me.

9

Making History

RAJ, AN INTERIOR designer and fitness coach, had run many ultra-races across India. Thanks to his clout with the running community, we had several runners who joined us over the thirty days. Raj had just returned from the Thar Desert Run on 13 April was suffering from high blood pressure. Despite the fact that he was the sole bread-winner of his family, he had left everything behind to be a part of this run.

Apurba Dass was an amazing ultra-runner. Nicknamed 'Old Monk' by us later during the run, Apurba had an easygoing personality that belied the hardships he had gone through in life. He held a modest railways job and had an ailing wife and a daughter to look after. His financial constraints held him back from participating in many races despite his commendable track record.

Sajjan Dabas was a former fashion designer who was now working in his family's construction business. He had a tough time convincing his father to let him participate and was out of work for a month of the run. Nicknamed 'Papa's Boy', he was already injured when he joined the run, and had to down banana shakes every day to boost his energy.

Mahesh worked as a guide with a travel company. Just before the run, he had been away from home on work for a month. He mostly kept to himself and rarely spoke to me unless Arvind was around. He had taken unpaid leave from work to join us.

All these men were veterans. They knew what to expect and exactly what could go wrong. I, of course, had no clue about what lay ahead.

We had all agreed to be a part of the initiative because we genuinely believed we could make a difference to the environment. The channel that had organized the event had promised to focus on the various initiatives that we would endorse on our way from Delhi to Mumbai, creating awareness among the millions of viewers across the country. Our stories of endurance and perseverance, as we tackled the harsh Indian roads, the pollution and the heat, would actually be for a good cause—raise money to help change life in the villages and towns affected by pollution and global warming. It was a moment, an occasion, that was so much bigger than us.

But the run happened in media silence and in obscurity.

The lone celebrity would eventually walk out with a car,

while the unnamed runners nursed their injuries and bruised egos.

It would be easy to pin the blame on the team leader, Milind Soman. The truth is, however, that he did try and salvage the situation.

But the event managers and the crew had only one agenda—TRP.

Day 1

20 April 2012

I had no clue of the perilous and dramatic race ahead when the alarm went off at 2.30 a.m. on 20 April 2012, day one of the run. I sprang up, packed my bags and applied petroleum jelly on my toes, chest and groin area to help reduce friction, got ready and headed downstairs to join the others. After a quiet, reflective breakfast, we stepped out into a pleasant morning to stretch and warm up.

I looked around. Everyone, other than Milind and me, was wearing new shoes. I was wearing my old Nikes, which had helped me win my first ultra-marathon. They are my lucky shoes and even though the cushioning has worn off, they remain my most prized possession.

Raj and Apurba were already cribbing about the crew. Apparently, last year's crew had been far more competent. It did not help that the crew arrived late at the spot and we had to rush ahead without our luggage.

We reached Qutub Minar with a few minutes to spare. We were all set to run. Around 4 a.m. we started our run. Live TV coverage was supposed to begin at 9.00 a.m., so we wanted to start running and cover some distance before returning to the venue for the official flag off before the media and other dignitaries.

One of the best things about this multiday run was that since this long distance had never been attempted before, there was no right or wrong strategy. The idea was to evolve and adapt as we moved along.

So while Milind and the others were planning to split the distances into stretches of 10 km, 8 km, 6 km and so on of continuous running with breaks, I had a different strategy.

It was evident that I wouldn't be able to match the guys in speed. So I planned to cover as much distance as I could and start walking whenever I got tired. With Arvind as my crew I had nothing to fear—I was in high spirits.

It was a great early morning run on empty roads. We ran for 15 km from Qutub Minar towards Gurgaon. By the time we came back, we had already clocked 30 km. What a boost it was to our confidence!

But there was also that friction on my right toe that made me sick in my guts. I never expected to finish the run with any toenails remaining, but I did not want the first one to go on the very first day of the run.

I learned my first lesson—for a long run, apply lubrication on your toes more liberally than usual. But nothing bothered me. By the time we finished our morning run, the crew had managed to get all our gear transferred to the bus accompanying us. I went inside, got a dressing done for my toe and changed into a new pair of shoes and socks. I was ready for more.

We were thrilled at the idea of being on TV and participating in something—especially a non-cricketing sport—that had such significance. The set-up was fairly elaborate. The team had a masseur, a doctor, a crew manager and a media unit of a recording manager and a cameraman, an assistant, an anchorwoman, another female crew member, a bus driver and three other drivers for the vehicles of the crew, including one only for me.

As I was getting down from the bus, I saw my parents and my brother waiting anxiously for me. We hugged as though we had found each other after several years. They had heard about my early injury and were worried about me.

My father was the most worried. 'Are you in pain? Do you have doubts about completing the run?' he asked me.

I smiled. I was in pain but not in doubt. 'No, Papa, I can easily do it. I'm very strong.'

My mother, the doctor, started giving me some health tips and safety measures to lighten the mood. 'Chinu, I am so proud of you. Just keep yourself hydrated and you won't get blisters.' Once again, it was a piece of advice I would eventually ignore and pay a heavy price for.

Papa seemed more concerned about the possibility of me quitting. 'Don't give up; don't let any negative thought stop you from reaching your goal. If you can then do more than 1,500 km, but a kilometre less is not acceptable. If you are in doubt, you can quit right now but do not quit once you leave Delhi. And remember, what doesn't kill you, only makes you stronger. We shall be waiting for you at the finishing line.'

His words stoked my ambition. It was time for the event to flag off. I glanced at my family waiting in the crowd. And then suddenly, we were rolling; we were live on national TV, where Milind introduced us and the run.

I waved to my family and hit the road, running.

The first encounter with the reality of the other India happened soon after we crossed Gurgaon. The highway was littered with broken beer and whisky bottles.

We had to run 15 km to reach the Bhatti Mines. The mines was to be our first environment stop.

Tucked away in a secret corner between Delhi and Haryana, Bhatti Mines was once a sad commentary on the construction boom that fed an illegal quarrying business. A massive afforestation programme over the last decade, however, has turned this place into a veritable haven, with lakes that fill up during the monsoon and myriad birds that flock there from various parts of the world. The mines are now a part of the Asola Sanctuary, with the remnants of the quarrying of the early days—the deep pits—now holding fresh water.

It was an oasis in the desert of the highway. The Territorial Army guys had done a commendable job of conservation indeed.

It was here that I also got to plant my first sapling. I had always seen celebrities do it and was thrilled to bits when I got an opportunity to do so myself and that too, before the camera. Only, thanks to a mix-up, my plant was labelled Mr Sumedha Mahajan!

Though we had clocked 45 km till now, I was prepared to clock 100 km. And when the men retired after 57 km, I decided to run further. This got Arvind out of the crew car to remind me that I had twenty-nine days to finish 1,500 km. I calculated—I had clocked 62 km that day. In any case, the traffic, the dust and pollution was getting worse and after a light drizzle there was a raging sandstorm that forced us to scrap our plans of running in the evening. After a shower, food and planning for the next day, I went off to sleep. In retrospect, it was my last night of sleeping in peace for the remaining days.

Day 2

I woke up feeling very tired, even though I had slept soundly. I took a bath and started getting ready, but my body felt unusually stiff.

I reasoned that the ache was probably because of yesterday's run around Bhatti Mines, but I somehow pulled myself together and joined the others at the lobby at 3.45 a.m. There I met Mala Honnatti. Raj introduced her as a mountaineer, skier and an ultra-runner who had completed the Everest base camp run, among other feats. She was there to support us; I couldn't believe how active and fit she was in her fifties.

Mala planned to run about 15–20 km with us and return. I was glad to have another woman, and an inspiring one like her, to run with.

At 4 a.m. sharp, we started off. Mala and I were running together. Thanks to yesterday's surprise rain in the evening, it was a pleasant morning with hardly any traffic.

But the moment I began to run, I knew something was not right.

I was running strongly but I was feeling drowsy. I was maintaining a decent pace, but it felt like I was dragging.

I had covered just 13 km. The other runners must have been 500 metres or more ahead of me. I was lagging behind. Mala was also 100–200 metres ahead of me. Only my crew was tailing me. It was still dark and soon, I lost sight of Mala as well.

I began to walk.

'Why did you stop running so early?' Arvind asked me from the vehicle.

'I want water and a banana,' I somehow managed to say.

After I had had the fruit and drank enough water, I pumped up the volume of my iPod and began walking again. But the drowsiness persisted. And at the 15-km mark, I fainted.

10

Shame

I OPENED MY eyes. Arvind was splashing water on my face.

There was something wet trickling down my legs. It was not sweat, but blood. I was down.

Arvind held me tight. 'It's okay, baby, you need to rest and clean yourself.' He got me a towel from the car and I cleaned myself bang in the middle of the road without giving a damn about who was watching me, all the while crying silently.

Arvind kept assuring me that everything was all right. But it wasn't.

I was convinced I was failing. And I hated it. It was shameful how I could not figure out that I was menstruating. That was the last thing I wanted to happen on the second day of the run. I was so busy running that I did not hear my body sending me warning signals.

But I did not have any time to waste. I somehow pulled myself together and tried to look for some sort of cover. There was nothing. There was only the road and trucks. With tears still streaming down my face, I used Arvind as my cover and dressed myself.

This was my first encounter with nature. I did get some unwanted attention, but I had no choice. I was embarrassed that I was being watched doing something so private.

In deep trauma, I asked the driver to take me back to the hotel. Arvind called up Raj and Apurba and told them about the change in my plan.

We reached the hotel in no time and I rushed to the bathroom, took a bath and tried to scrub off the memories of the horrific scene from my entire being. I tried to gather enough strength to get back on the road.

After a change of clothes, I was back to my old self. I was raring to go. But my husband wouldn't hear any of it.

Raj, our fitness expert had advised him to give me oral hydration liquids and glucose. I hate the taste of ORS, but under orders from Arvind I had three glasses and a sandwich and went off to sleep.

I learned my first and most crucial lesson that day—always listen to your body.

I woke up at 10 a.m. and realized I was running out of time. Even as I hurriedly got ready, Arvind pleaded with me to take a day off. He had become quite emotional but I wanted to run and make up for the lost time. Besides, there was no room for pain or discomfort on this race.

Our discussion turned into a bitter, heated argument. 'I have had enough of clarity,' I thundered. 'I am a woman, Arvind, and people expect me to fail and give up. What I am going through is something every woman goes through. And please understand, I do not want to finish with a consolation prize of participation, but finish shoulder to shoulder with the men. I just have to run today.'

I looked into Arvind's eyes. He was ready to let me go.

11

Some Wounds Don't Heal

THE PRESSURE OF the remaining kilometres kept building up on me. By the time I met the other runners around lunchtime, they had completed the morning quota of 50 km and planned to top it up with another 5–10 km in the evening.

I put on a brave face when they asked me about my condition. But I was worried about having done only 75 km when they had clocked 100.

But I was feeling refreshed after my morning rest and that afternoon, managed to run 25 km. I was now lagging behind by 11 km. I shared my concerns with Raj.

'I'm sorry I let you down,' I told him. 'I didn't expect this to happen. I am mentally strong but my body is weak. I wanted to run longer but I just couldn't do it.'

Raj consoled me, 'Just look at this way; you will need to

run 1 km more than us for the next eleven days. It's not a big deal. But today I saw true sportsmanship. Remember it's not a competition and you are not a laggard. You need to complete the run and there are twenty-eight more days to go.'

I was happy to hear him speak so highly of me, but when Milind called me on my cell phone, I immediately went on the defensive; I thought he was calling to ask me to leave the race. However, he laughed it off. 'You have done 102 km in two days which is 2 km more than the required average. So you are doing a great job,' he said encouragingly. 'If I had any doubts about your performance I wouldn't have invited you for the run in the first place.'

Buoyed and confident, I went back to my room where Arvind was waiting for me, anxiety writ large on his face.

'This is just the beginning, baby. You need to take care of yourself.'

'I'll be fine...trust me,' I said with my most reassuring tone. But I knew things were not entirely in my control. If today was bad, things were about to get worse.

Day 3

I was awake at 2.30 a.m. As was my routine for this run, I began by applying petroleum jelly on my body to reduce the friction with my clothes. And that's when I noticed painful chafing on my breasts.

When I called on the crew doctor and asked him for some medicinal tape or cotton gauze, he said he was not carrying any.

What was more shocking was that despite being the doctor on call for the marathon, he was not carrying things that were essential for such an undertaking; even a simple Band-Aid was missing from his so-called kit. None of the runners were carrying a medical kit, assuming the doctor would have been prepared with everything we would need on the way.

This led to somewhat of an uproar, as we wondered, rather loudly, what the doctor was doing in the team with us in the first place. Thankfully, the hotel staff was better equipped. I borrowed some regular tapes and cotton and plastered my lacerations—I used them as it could at least prevent further lacerations or so I thought. This was to turn out to be a big mistake later.

After our customary session of tea, bananas and biscuits and a brief chat about the plan for the day, I started off by kissing the ground beneath my feet, thanking my guardian angels and waving at Arvind who was in my tracking car. The other runners were well within sight, the sun was rising and there was a powdery drizzle.

I love running in the rain. Considering the hot Indian summer, these were dream conditions for runners. But strange as it may sound, I had never seen a rainbow...until then. It was majestic and an almost 180-degree one.

I called out to Arvind, pointing at the rainbow. We both knew it was the sign of good luck and a new beginning I so badly needed. I managed to run 45 km that day and walked for another 5 km.

We got off the highway and later drove to a little village where I grabbed a lot of eyeballs for my so-called masculine attire. In the interiors of Rajasthan, I realized I created a flutter because of what I was doing and the way I looked.

Rajasthan has always been a conservative state, though it is a top tourist attraction. Other than the beautiful palaces and forts, there is something else that strikes you about it—on the highways and in the villages too, you hardly get to see any women. Even if you do, they would be dressed in ghagras, their heads and faces covered with a dupatta. The veil and female infanticide continue to exist in Rajasthan, which has also, till very recently, extolled the virtues of a sati—a woman who jumped into the funeral pyre of her husband. I was running across a state where the birth of a girl child was considered to be a curse.

While the other people in the team were busy, I managed to have a chat with the women in the village. They were shocked to know that a married woman could actually run and even wear such clothes.

The men were confused, too. Several times I overheard them debating if I was an Indian or a foreigner. The general consensus was that since I was wearing shorts, I must be a foreigner. I was both sad and happy—sad because of their ignorance, and happy because I was breaking fiercely held gender stereotypes.

For a country that worships and promotes only cricket, the state of other sports is pathetic. It is even worse for women. I am not a professional athlete, but knowing the travails of those women who are, I was not really surprised at the responses I elicited.

I was pensive on the way back to the hotel, where some bad news awaited me.

The doctor said he could not get medicinal tape anywhere and that we had to wait until Jaipur to get it. I sighed, threw up my hands and went up to my room. But before that, I managed to get hold of some Band-Aid, which seemed more desirable than a Louis Vuitton bag at that moment.

I stepped into the shower and tried to take off the tape on my breasts. The simple task had become more painful than I had imagined and I let them be.

We ran some more in the evening, but the roads were getting dustier, and after 10 km, we called it a day. I rushed to the bathroom and started to remove the tapes again. It proved to be extremely painful. I tried wetting the tapes, ripping them out slowly and then yanking them off in one go. I wanted to cry out, but didn't want to scare my husband. I stuffed a towel into my mouth, gritted my teeth and pulled them out. One painful bit by another.

The lacerations were now too big for Band-Aid. I somehow managed to clean them, slathered some oil and stepped out with a smile pasted on my face.

While Arvind was getting ready, I was desperately trying to figure out ways and means to make him stay back. I knew my lacerations would worsen by the time we reached Jaipur.

I wanted him to be around to take care of me.

Dinner was in the lawns of the hotel and the mood was cheerful. But I was restive, which Arvind noticed. Just as we all noticed how the crew sat at a different table, away from the runners. Eating together, laughing together, brings about better synergy. But they didn't seem to think so.

Day 4

It was 1 a.m. and Arvind was all packed and dressed to leave for Mumbai. We were currently 100 km away from Jaipur, but planned to reach Jaipur today. Arvind called for a cab to take him to the Jaipur airport. He kissed my forehead. I started crying. 'Why can't you stay for another day? You know I'm not well. I need you. I cannot do it without you. Please...I'm begging you! I'm sorry for my bad health. I will not fall sick again. Please stay,' I sobbed like a little girl.

Arvind hugged me tight and said soothingly, 'Baby, I can't. I have to report to work. I have responsibilities I cannot run away from. At least one of us needs to maintain a steady job. I know you can manage but I am mad at you because you don't take care of your health.'

'You think I like falling sick?'

'I'm sorry, I know it's not your fault but it hurts to see you sick and running alone in this heat. It's going to make me mad!' Arvind could not hide the hurt in his eyes.

'When you know I'm running alone shouldn't you stay with me? I cannot do without you!'

'It kills me to leave you in pain. I know everyone is running and fighting their own battles but I can only feel your pain. Baby, just take care. I will be with you in Ajmer. I cannot take leave from work. One of us has to earn a living.'

I realized I was being unreasonable. I had taken a huge risk with my professional life by running for this event. Arvind had to be the practical one. 'Leave before I get weak again,' I sighed and kissed him goodbye.

12

The Devil Returns

ARVIND LEFT ME in the empty room with just my thoughts for company.

I looked at myself in the mirror.

I saw a girl, a daughter and a wife. A daughter who had taken up an immense challenge with the blessings of her parents; a wife who had her husband by her side when she challenged her own limits; and a girl who was now left all alone to deal with uncertainties and loneliness.

'Be strong, carry on,' I kept saying to myself as I dressed up, taped my wounds again, packed my bags and checked out.

At 3 a.m. it was too early for me to start running. But when I called up the crew manager and told him about my plans, he was clearly taken aback.

'It's not a good idea for a woman to run in the dark on

the highway, and that, too, alone. We will allow you to run only when everyone else starts,' he said peremptorily.

I was unwilling to give up. 'You don't understand. I am lagging behind and I have to cover the gap. I'm just starting an hour before the men. Besides I will have a tracking vehicle behind me as well as your team, so I won't really be alone.'

'Sorry, we cannot allow you to run now.'

'What if I go 3 km ahead and come back 3 km is that fine? Is that fine?'

He was quiet for a bit and replied, 'Let me think about it and find out if any of the crew members are willing to step out now.'

A few minutes later, he called me to say I could start running.

I ran for 3 km and returned to the start point, making up the 6 km of the 11-km lag. I felt calmer.

In the hotel, I saw Milind attending to his missing toenail. I looked at the others; each of us was nursing some injury or the other. It was a battlefront, where everyone was in pain but bravely soldiered on.

I began with the rest at a good pace. But as the sun climbed higher, the traffic got worse, as did the pollution.

It was getting difficult for me to breathe. I was sneezing often and could hear a wheezing sound with every breath that I took.

It was back—the tormentor from my childhood. And I could not deny it any longer.

Cursing my luck and struggling to keep the attack at bay, I tried to run as far as possible without taking any medication. But I could sense my body and my lungs giving up. After 30 km, I was completely breathless. I walked, tried to run, but couldn't. I stopped my vehicle, took a few puffs from my inhaler and tried to run again. But after barely 500 metres, I started coughing violently and reached out for it again.

My teammates had long left me behind. I grabbed a handkerchief, covered my mouth and nose and started running.

I realized that this run was going to be tough to finish. Now, it was not just about injuries, but something much worse.

13

The Tortoise and the Rabbit

AT THE 35-KM mark I saw the other runners taking a break and having their refreshments. Milind and Raj waved at me and were shouting my name to come and have some refreshments but I could not even waste any time. Every breath of mine was heavy and precious—I knew I had to run for the next 15 km. The next stretch, the last one to the hotel, was perhaps the toughest of my life. I walked and ran and kept using my inhaler after every 3–4 km but still kept moving forward. I was slow, but I knew I could not give up till I had covered my day's quota.

After clocking 50 km, I crumbled on the road and lay there. I was exhausted and hygiene was the last thing on my mind.

My crew vehicle stopped next to me and one of the crew members ran towards me.

'Are you okay? Why don't you call it off and rest?'

I smiled, despite the panting. 'Simply because everyone expects me to do so. I am not calling it quits,' I managed. In my mind, I was the proverbial tortoise. *Slow and steady wins the race.*

I finally reached the hotel. I was satisfied but completely beat. Excusing myself from the day's activity, I rushed to my room for my dose of nebulization. The time for the inhaler was long gone.

On a normal day, the nebulizer would have been effective, but not today. My biggest fears were slowly turning true. I could sense the onset of a massive attack. I began to worry about the remaining kilometres. Could it get any worse? I wondered. My body was revolting—periods, asthma, blisters, cramps... and I had another twenty-six days to go.

I quickly reworked my strategy—I would run when the asthma was manageable and start an hour before everyone else. I figured that my daily headstart would ensure that at the end of the day, I was at par with the others.

I felt better, and was about to doze off when I realized I had not spoken to my husband. We had decided to speak to each other at least once every day.

I saw a text from Arvind. He had reached the office. I was dying to talk to him but I was scared to call him. He would know immediately that I had had an asthma attack. He was already tense when he left and I didn't want to add to his anxiety. But if I didn't call him, he would get worried and call up the other runners for an update on how I was doing.

I decided to keep it short. 'It was a good run but I need to sleep now,' I said. He didn't press me for details and I was grateful for his restraint as I didn't want sympathy right then. All I needed was confidence. But I knew that he knew I was having an asthma attack.

I tried to sleep but I couldn't. I had another attack and took another round of nebulization. Raj called to check on me. 'How are you? Arvind called to tell me you are not well. He has asked me to take care of you. You are like a child to me, so please call me when you need anything, okay?' he said reassuringly.

I could not talk properly as I was using the nebulizer. I replied in a hoarse voice, 'I'll be fine, please don't worry. What time are we starting in the evening?'

Raj still sounded worried, 'Please rest in the evening. Don't run. Do you need a doctor?'

I quickly replied, 'I will run in the evening, no matter what happens. I have already skipped once. If I skip again, every time I face a challenge I will feel like doing so.'

Raj sounded a little more relaxed, and said, 'I love your spirit. Why don't you come down and we will have lunch and tea together?'

How was my body reacting to the grind that I was putting it through?

My periods were longer than usual and I was feeling weak. I had blisters on my toes and my toenails were getting blacker. My chest condition was worsening and my rashes were spreading. The older wounds looking a vibrant purple. I had no time to feel sorry for myself but had to act immediately.

I punctured my blisters and dipped my feet in cold water. I applied whatever antiseptic lotion the crew could provide and got ready.

Only, Jaipur was another day away and I was worried about my congestion.

I went to meet Raj and Apurba in the room they were sharing. All the runners were exhausted and no one had the energy to walk down to the restaurant. Raj was also in pain. He had injured his right leg and was applying an ointment. Apurba had heard from Raj about my condition and was concerned about me. There was still a bit of wheezing in my breath and though they insisted that I take some rest, I wouldn't hear any of it.

It was then that I finally got to know Apurba well. He spoke about his humble background, his fight with depression and financial problems and how running liberated him.

A fellowship was formed that day—I had two paternal figures taking care of me. The three of us would share our meals and stories till the end. The other runners, Mahesh and Sajjan, were together most of the time. And in the last few days of the race, Mahesh preferred to spend more time with Milind. And though we were slowly aligning ourselves to people we got along with, Milind ensured that all the runners sat together for at least one meal every day.

I felt a lot better in the evening, and to be on the safe side, had taken a preventive dose of nebulization before the run. Raj had advised me to tie a wet handkerchief around my mouth to help me breathe in these polluted conditions.

It helped, but at that time, I realized how important it was to have cleaner air in India. I wanted to run for the cause more desperately, but I decided not to push very hard and finished the evening run at an even pace.

After the evening run, I requested a female crew member to examine my breasts. When she saw the extent of the lacerations, she freaked out.

14

My Body Beautiful

IT WAS A mistake sharing my condition with the woman. She seemed hell bent on getting me off the tracks.

She said, 'Sumedha, you have to stop running immediately! We cannot take such a huge risk with your condition.'

I suppressed my anger and calmly told her, 'We will be in Jaipur tomorrow. We will go to a hospital and let the doctors take a call. I'm tired and need to sleep.'

I shrugged her off and went to my room.

I lay there, thinking about my condition. I was getting stronger in my mind, but my body was getting weaker. I was clearly losing my appetite. My diet was only tea and biscuits, which was certainly not helping me. Other runners like Apurba, Mahesh and Sajjan, were eating voraciously, gorging on rice, banana milkshakes and pulses. Perhaps it was the reason they didn't suffer as much.

I got up, ordered some dal and rice and felt good after polishing it all off. I decided to take care of my diet and eat even when my body complained of exhaustion. Looking back, it was one of the most important decisions that helped me survive under those conditions.

At night my breasts continued to hurt. I took a dose of nebulization again, but spent another sleepless night.

Day 5

Next morning, my breasts were hurting more than ever. I went to the bathroom to get ready for the run and I examined myself. There were bloodstains on my T-shirt.

I took it off. My breasts were completely infected. The nipples were bruised and bleeding.

I was tanned. There were dark circles under my eyes. I had not lost weight yet but I felt lighter than before. My toenails were either black or had fallen off. There were blisters on my feet and ankles.

I quickly got the first-aid kit from the hotel reception and patched myself up to the best of my ability. When I applied antiseptic on my breasts, they hurt like hell. I yelled and cried, collapsing on the bathroom floor. I dragged myself out of the bathroom, struggling to take a breath, fighting the pain in my breasts, and reached for the nebulizer. When my breathing had normalized, I lay back on the floor, trying to reassure myself. 'I'm with you. There, there...'

I had no confidence in the doctor who was accompanying us. He was utterly useless. My only hope was in Jaipur, where I was sure we'd get a proper doctor.

I looked at the clock and realized it was already 3 a.m. Time to move fast. I pulled myself together and got ready. I stepped out confidently. But when I approached my vehicle, I realized the crew already knew about my breast infection.

Instead of appreciating my willpower, they began to discourage me. It seemed as though I was simply a liability for them. I hated that feeling. I wanted to scream at them, but realized it would be futile.

This was a motley crew of media professionals, none of whom ran or had any idea of running, except for the fact that some of them wore running shoes.

I wonder why my crew was so inconsiderate towards me. Was it because I had stopped wearing the official T-shirt that they had stopped covering me? Or was it because I was slow and always falling sick and they had to start early and finish late for me?

Though I was the lone woman in the team and going through such extreme conditions, they never encouraged or empathized with me. They treated me as a burden they'd rather let go of.

The only person they had eyes for was Milind. I realized they were no more than star-struck kids and forgave them.

Luckily, my driver was more supportive and I started my run towards Jaipur.

Jaipur is known for being a marble hub, and as you approach the beautiful city, you can see the roads dotted with marble shops where workers cut and polish the stones, sending up clouds of marble dust into the air. To top it all, the highway had massive infrastructure projects going on, making the conditions extremely unsuitable for running. Especially for an asthmatic patient like me.

But today, early in the morning, thanks to the less polluted air, running was easy. The roads too, were fairly empty. But once the sun started climbing higher, I began to sweat.

It felt as though someone was rubbing salt on my breast wounds.

It was pure torture.

I wanted to shout, cry, stop and give up. I tried to ignore the pain but I couldn't stop my tears. I let them flow and just concentrated on my goal of reaching Jaipur. I decided to run for 2 km and walk for 1 km.

My fellow runners overtook me, shouting words of encouragement. 'Come on, Sumedha! Well done, Sumedha! You can do it.' It was the sweetest sound I had heard since morning.

Around noon, I was still 10 km away from the destination. My breathing became heavy again. I immediately stopped the vehicle and puffed on my inhaler. My breasts were hurting and bleeding and because of the sweat, the stains were prominent.

Giving up was not even an option. The next 10 km turned out to be the longest, hardest and most painful I had ever run.

I started singing out loud to distract myself. As if by some divine intervention my playlist started playing my favourite poem:

Vriksh ho bhale kadhe
Ho ghane ho bade
Ek patt chaawn ki
Maang matt maang matt
Agneepath agneepath.

(Trees around you may be big and strong, but do not ask for shelter,
Keep walking on the path of fire, keep walking on the path of fire.)

The immortal and powerful lines by the legendary poet Harivanshrai Bachchan always give me strength and hope, and I kept singing out loud and running ahead. I looked up. I could see only empty roads with a few trucks diving by. I looked around me and I saw only barren land. I was alone.

I kneeled down on the road, wanting to fall asleep right there.

My driver, Pritam, a man in his forties, who was always concerned about me, got off the vehicle and came up to me. 'Did you have to take up this project of killing yourself in the desert with me forced to follow you around at this annoyingly slow pace? I don't even get to sleep properly. You wake me up earlier than the other drivers are called,' he said scathingly.

This run was tough for him as well. Driving the car for so many days in the heat and pressing the clutch and brake every few minutes' work hard on the legs.

I smiled and said, 'Just a few more days, sir, and then you can sleep the entire day.' He went back to the car and banged the door shut.

We were stuck together until the end. No amount of crying or complaining would help.

Somehow, despite everything falling apart, I managed to finish my last 10 km. As soon as we reached Jaipur, I was rushed to the hospital.

15

A Shot at Hope

I HAD RAISED hell with the organizers for not providing us with an efficient doctor in the crew. As a result, they scrambled to get me to the Fortis Hospital, where a doctor was waiting for me. He examined me and was shocked at what he saw. 'This is the worst case of chafing I have ever come across,' he said, shaking his head, and asked me how I had injured myself this way. When I told him my story, he looked at me differently.

He re-examined my breasts and said, 'It is not as bad as it looks. Luckily, you came here just in time, before the infection could penetrate the skin. Right now, it's still on the surface. But seriously, I'm awestruck at how you managed to hold yourself together through this; it's remarkable!'

The doctor dressed my wounds, prescribed some medicines and ointment, urged me to take ample precautions and then let me go, but not before adding, 'The wounds will take at least twenty days to heal. I am shocked at how the so-called crew doctor gave you ordinary tapes. Had your condition been addressed on day one, you would not have been here.' I shot a triumphant look at the crew member accompanying me.

That was not all. When the doctor realized that despite his note of caution, I was determined to complete the run without anymore breaks, he arranged for a specialist to check on my asthma. It was a blessing, as the doctor gave me medications to arrest recurring attacks.

On my way out of the hospital, I saw a small crowd of doctors and nurses waiting to catch a glimpse of me. I was told that my story had had spread through the hospital and I was the cause of some intrigue among the medical staff, but not in the way I would have liked. 'Why are you doing this?' 'Is it worth risking so much?' They all had the same questions. My heart sank. What answer could I possibly give? What could I say that would explain my reasons my actions, my endeavours to rank strangers? What motivated me, made me push myself to the limit of my endurance? It's not something anyone could have ever understood, except my family or perhaps my fellow runners.

Thankfully, I was feeling a lot better physically. I quickly exited the hospital and reached my hotel to update Raj and Apurba—my loyal comrades who were fighting with the organizers about how they could as even think of asking me to leave. It was their mis-management that had brought in an inefficient doctor as our crew. Both of them ensured that they motivated me enough and never let even a grain of doubt creep in regarding my ability to complete the run. They were relieved to hear about the doctor's verdict and glad to know that I can run with them.

Arvind was not in the least bit surprised when I finally came clean about my breast wounds and what had happened.

Apparently, he had been in touch with Raj all the time. He also said that the crew had called him up to request me to stop running.

'They told me you aren't fit to run and I should take you home,' he said.

I was not furious at the crew for speaking behind my back to my husband but I was tense, wondering if Arvind also had lost faith in me and had changed his mind.

'What did you tell them?' I asked.

'I said that instead of asking you to stop running, they should arrange for a proper doctor to attend to you. And in case they were incapable of doing so, I would organize a specialist myself.'

I bit my lips as a surge of emotions overtook me.

'Baby,' continued my husband reassuringly. 'Don't listen to them; just keep running...you're doing well...just stay away from the crew. I will see you in Ajmer.'

Now, I was more determined than ever to finish the run—come what may.

To become a fighter, you need to learn an important lesson—

how to channel both encouragement and discouragement towards enhancing your performance. During those last few days of pain and suffering, I learned to work with both.

The run, which had started as an environmental initiative and to set a new record, was now more than that. It had become a battle. When you are alone, you come face-to-face with two powerful energies—your inner strength and your inner weakness. I chose my inner strength.

But things were not quite all right with my comrades.

In the evening, I noticed Raj grimacing in pain as he limped through his run.

I caught up with him when he stopped to catch his breath. He had tendonitis, a painful condition for athletes. But his face or voice did not betray any emotions.

Raj could not run, so he just walked. I joined him to give him some moral support.

The next day we would have soldiers from the Jaipur army team join us, as well as Raj's friend, Deepak. Since there were no proper hotels for the next 50–100 km, it was decided that we would stay in the hotel for two nights, do our daily running, and come back to the hotel. Given the inhospitable condition of the Indian highways, it seemed to be the most pragmatic thing to do. This is why most of the ultra-marathons across the world are run in loops, so that the runners can be provided with proper facilities.

Considering the stress that runners go through, basic comfort was the least that one could have expected from the organizers. But this was obviously turning out to be a point of contention between the runners and the crew, and despite the fun and games planned for us by the crew, I could sense tempers getting frayed and mercury levels rising.

The long and eventful day ended with a cultural evening the crew had planned for us. I was feeling confident and happy to have been able to get professional help for my injuries. It was working better than medicines. I sang and danced my heart away.

Day 6, dawned on a positive note.

The new doctor who had joined us was young and resourceful. He was enthusiastic as well. When I returned to my hotel after my usual morning run, I found my team waiting for me.

I could feel the pain for me in their eyes, thinking how they had veered away from supporting me and encouraging me—it was my battle and I had to fight it alone. First, Milind came and hugged me. And then one by one, everyone else—except Mahesh—followed. We laughed and we were teary-eyed, suddenly realizing how we were all in it together.

And today, especially, I was not alone.

Raj's friend Deepak began to run with me. We struck up a rapport as Deepak regaled me with stories of his adventures around the world. But at the 35-km mark we saw Raj carrying on gingerly.

He was obviously in a lot of pain. His condition had worsened. I decided to walk with him. Not used to the pace,

Raj was walking slower than usual. But we egged each other on and aimed to get to a 6-7-km-per-hour pace. I was feeling stronger and optimistic and feeling good about not running alone.

In the evening, Raj and I were running at an easy pace, when I suddenly developed cramps in my calves. Despite his own condition, Raj stopped to help me work out the cramps and we finished the day with one-fifth of the target completed—and a deeper, stronger bond between us.

16

New Bonds

Day 7

After two days of civilization, we were back in the wild as we left for Kishangarh. A city in the Ajmer district, it is the birthplace of a distinctive and beautiful style of painting. But now it has earned the dubious moniker of the marble capital of the country—thanks to the thriving industry centred on the stone. You can also imagine what it does to the air and our bodies. I had made up my mind about two things—not to run alone and to keep my distance from negativity.

So I waited to join Raj in the morning run. We decided to run for 500 metres and walk for 500. The other runners overtook us, shouting words of encouragement.

By the time the sun was up, we had crossed the polluting

marble factories. The barren lands were rendered beautiful with many birds and the occasional peacock enjoying the harsh sun, unmindful about human presence, even though the unrelenting sun did nothing to help us.

For Raj, nothing seemed to work. His swelling had increased. He requested for ice, but the crew did not have any. He used towels soaked in cold drinking water instead and almost disappeared behind a cloud of relaxant sprays.

Watching Raj struggling through his pain, I realized each one of us were making immense sacrifices to complete the run.

By then, we had almost become like machines—wake up, run, eat, sleep, run, dip feet in ice water, sleep, repeat. Only Mahesh and Sajjan got their legs massaged by the masseur travelling with us. The other men avoided this after the masseur gave a sprain to Milind by pressing some wrong nerve. I avoided the masseur as he was male.

In the evening, I wanted to run with Raj again. Running in the dark was always dangerous, especially with the terrible driving of Indian motorists. Unfortunately, we were not provided with reflective strips nor could we procure the same in the middle of the run. But as we were about to leave, our new doctor, Arun, said he wanted to join us and we happily agreed. The young doctor ran with us for a while and returned, but not before promising us to regroup the next morning to run together again. It just felt wonderful to know that we were touching lives, inspiring rank strangers to join us and our cause.

But as for the crew, it was obvious that the rift between them and the runners was widening. Since Raj was a fitness expert, Milind had entrusted him with the task of looking after the runners and their fitness requirements. This brought him in direct confrontation with the inept crew put together by the media house.

'There is not enough ice in the cars. We are getting injured every day,' Raj argued with the crew. 'You throw attitude at us if we ask for assistance but can't provide us with the most basic things!'

'If you runners are not fit, why did you sign up for this? All of you were aware of your conditions,' the crew manager shot back.

The situation was pretty dismal. Every day I wished some senior person would visit us and review our progress, but that never happened. The crew members were not clued into the expectations of their bosses from day one. And it remained that way.

It had become plainly obvious that the crew, put together hurriedly and without much thought, was not interested in sports or this run.

But I had stopped expecting anything from the crew, and as advised by Arvind, decided to maintain a studied distance from the negativity.

After that evening's run, I sat outside the hotel with Milind, Sajjan, Raj and Apurba. It was a full-moon night and a cool breeze was blowing. This was one of the few moments when we were out in the open, not doing any physical activity; just relaxing.

We had our dinner outside under the stars. It was a perfect evening and we went to bed late, at 10 p.m. While the men had their food and beer, I deviated from my daily schedule of dal and rice and decided to treat myself to some rotis.

That turned out to be a huge mistake.

17

What Crap!

Day 8

I woke up with an upset tummy.

I had to do a bathroom run three times before leaving the room. I figured it was the rotis from the previous night that were the culprits. I popped in medicine for an upset tummy and went outside to begin the run.

We had run only 8 km when my stomach started rumbling again. I asked Raj to go ahead and scan the area for a cover.

I was in the middle of nowhere. There was no shrub, tree or even a building behind which I could relieve myself.

A little further away, I saw a small bush and without wasting any time, I grabbed a bottle of water, some tissues and relieved myself. The bush was barely enough to cover me, and

I knew people were watching me, but I did not care because I had no choice. I kept telling myself that no one would know who it was since my face was covered with a handkerchief and sunglasses.

By the time I reached the destination where the others were waiting after the morning run, I had already relieved myself four times on the highway.

I was beat when I reached the hotel. But that, it turned out, was not going to be the end of my suffering.

When I stepped in for a shower, I realized my nose was bleeding. The diarrhoea, heat and dust were taking a toll on me. I called room service for ice, put ice on my head and drank a few glasses of buttermilk before crashing.

By evening, when I joined Raj and Apurba for our run, my stomach felt better but my nose was still bleeding. I saw Sajjan running with Mahesh, who was getting fitter every day. I felt a twinge of bitterness. I wanted to be fit and healthy like them.

Day 9

My condition was considerably better than the day before and I needed to take fewer breaks during the run. I still went in the great outdoors to relieve myself, without any shame. I was okay with enduring the glances and comments rather than cause discomfort to my body. It was going through much suffering in any case.

We reached the hotel in the afternoon and I saw Arvind waiting for me in the lobby. I couldn't contain myself and ran towards him, showering him with kisses like a child. He seemed embarrassed with my public show of love and chided me affectionately.

For my part, I was not in the least bothered by his embarrassment.

18

Right Side of Wrong

ARVIND WAS WORRIED sick when he saw me rush to the loo every now and then.

He insisted on checking the extent of my injuries himself. I hesitated to undress and show him my bruised body; I was feeling shy, ashamed and scared, all at once. But after a great deal of persuasion from Arvind, I undressed slowly.

I was bruised, tanned and bleeding.

He held his breath for a while and held on to me tenderly, tearfully. His reassuring touch was all that I needed to forget the torture I had been inflicting on myself.

Arvind had assumed it would be easier to arrange for a doctor in Ajmer and he called one of the crew members for help. He was not prepared for their retort.

An argument ensued and Arvind lost his cool. 'You cannot

treat her like crap,' he yelled and flung the phone away.

He looked at me helplessly.

'Baby, has the crew been rude to you?'

I was quiet. I did not want him to get drawn into the ugliness.

I tried to reason. 'They are from a non-sporting background. They do not understand how tough this route and run can be for a woman. They are tired following us around. This is something they have never done before.'

'Do you know what he said? He said, "Ask her to go home if she can't run." What do they think of themselves?'

I tried my best to remain calm. 'I'm not a kid who needs to complain about other people's conduct. Besides, we have no clue about how media organizations function. Maybe for them, Milind is the only runner. I am of no use to them, just a part of the side show. I don't really blame them.'

'We should complain to the top management about this conduct,' Arvind thundered.

'What's the point? I will miss the run.'

But Arvind was still angry and upset. 'What about the runners other than Milind? Is it bad for them as well?'

Much as I hated to admit it, I quietly nodded.

'I just don't understand you guys. If it is so bad, why are you even running? Why don't you boycott the run and raise your voice? Being rude is misconduct and not part of any job in the world. If it is only about TRPs, then only Milind should run and you guys should all pack up your bags and go home.'

'We are in the middle of nowhere and we are forced to find our own solutions. If I were to listen to your advice and quit, who would stand to lose? I would. And in the end I will validate their point that I can't run. I didn't sign up for this run thinking that it's going to be cakewalk.'

Arvind was quiet.

I continued, 'We all are focused on running and spreading the message. Period. Getting emotional and cribbing will get us nowhere. There will be a time and place when I will speak out. The race has just begun and we have twenty-one days left.'

Arvind looked down and said, 'I hope you get your chance.'

'I will. I want to rest and get ready for the evening run.'

Arvind went down for lunch and tried talking to a few of the crew members about the lack of coverage on TV.

Till he joined us, we had no clue about what was happening in the real world. We were mostly staying in hotels that did not air that particular news channel or were too tired to turn on the TVs. But Arvind had found out that for an event that was designed and attempted to create new records, the coverage was appallingly poor. After the fifteen minutes of airtime at the beginning of the event, it was reduced to a ticker on the left side of the screen with the number of kilometres covered and the rare thirty-second footage of Milind only.

But the crew members were uncomfortable discussing the issue, saying that the decision was their seniors. They also claimed that the event was not generating enough TRPs despite their daily uploads. And they did not have a clue why.

They also dropped another bomb. Due to low TRPs and high costs, they had been forced to cut back on the crew. So the live links were stopped, one vehicle was sent back and all social events were scrapped too. Without any live coverage for the social activities, we were not enticed to sacrifice our precious rest time in any case. But the strange thing was that they retained the fuel-guzzling bus, which was only used as a transportation vehicle. They said they wanted it for visibility and promoting the event. Well, the bus was never with the runners. It was most of the times parked at the hotels where we were put up, and it was the only vehicle which had posters and stickers about the event. Strangely the cars that followed us all the time didn't have any poster or sticker about the event on them. They were just another vehicle on the highway.

It soon emerged that it was not just the runners who were unhappy. There were reasons for the crew to be bitter as well.

This was a month-long event. The team was from the special projects division, young and eager to get noticed and make significant inroads in their careers.

But with no coverage on television, the internet or any other social media, their efforts were going completely unnoticed.

The runners at least would be credited for completing the 1,500 km; they would get nothing. And it was their frustration that was colouring their perception of us. It was a really sad situation.

So while the runners and the crew members were trying to come to terms with the unfairness of it all, the run continued at its regular pace. That evening, Raj called me down to begin our evening leg of the run. My husband was relieved to see how considerate all runners were towards me—even Mahesh, who was usually a little distant, for reasons unknown. And this is how the turnaround happened.

We were close to Ajmer Sharif; I had beautiful memories of the dargah from my childhood, when I had visited with my family. I was back in Ajmer with my husband, and I secretly wished I could revisit the shrine. As if reading my mind, Mahesh suddenly asked everyone if we wanted to visit the dargah. When I suggested that it may be too crowded, Mahesh simply smiled and said, 'Leave that to me.' It was the first time that I had a pleasant and complete conversation with him. Around 8 p.m., after our run, we regrouped. Some of the runners opted out, but Arvind and I, and a few of the crew members joined Mahesh as he led us to the dargah. Thanks to his tourism job, he had developed a rapport with the maulvis and treated us to the most beautiful experience at the shrine. We met again in Milind's room, to have dinner as we had missed the team lunch.

We were sitting around chatting and tending to our injuries, making light of our challenges. It was heartening to see how with every incident, we seemed to get closer, friendlier. We gave nicknames to each other—Apurba was the 'Old monk who runs like Ferrari'; Raj was 'Bruce Lee'; I was 'Iron Lady'; Sajjan was 'Papa's Boy'; Milind was 'Captain Vyom' and Mahesh was 'Zombie'.

19

Change Is in the Air

Day 10

With Arvind by my side, I felt stronger than ever. But over the next couple of days, my health swung like a pendulum—from being fit to fragile and often crumbling under asthma attacks. We ran to Barar in the heat and alongside the smoke-spewing trucks.

My speed was good today even though I was doing more walking than running. Eventually, my walk had improved. While the others finished their 50 km by 11 a.m., I knew I had to push on till 1 p.m.

I was completely exhausted and I slept in the vehicle on our way to the hotel. I was waking up from a deep slumber when we reached the hotel. It took me some time to even realize where I was. I had pushed myself very hard on this day. I had a massive asthma attack again today just when I reached the room and I had to take nebulization twice to become normal.

My appetite was dying and eating food was becoming hard day-by-day. Somehow, I forced some food down and slept.

I was feeling much better in the evening and I planned to run 15 km instead of 10 km. And by end of the day I had completed 565 km.

Day 11. 30 April, we were at the beautiful Aravallis.

The heat now was intolerable, sapping every ounce of energy from our bodies. Arvind insisted on getting out of the car to walk with me and take pictures to cheer me up. We also saw Deepak standing in the middle of nowhere. Since he was a guest runner, the crew insisted that he make his own arrangements and refused to give him any water or nourishment. It was a really unfortunate incident and would soon return to haunt all of us, in an uglier avatar.

But right now, we were drunk on the beauty of one of the oldest mountain ranges in the world.

Whether it was plains, deserts or mountain ranges, the one thing the runners couldn't complain about was getting bored with the landscape. We were now crossing the most beautiful stretches of the Aravalli range. At a different time of the year, the run would have been so much more enjoyable, but now the hot and dry weather played truant. Being able to get away from the bigger cities sensitized us to the fact that the roads were less crowded and dusty, and there was more greenery and beauty to feast our eyes on.

I felt more connected with nature than ever before. Instead of worrying about the heat, I chose to welcome the sunlight and the blisteringly hot days felt cooler than before; trees on the roadside waited to give me shade and the peaks quietly watched me like wise old men, at times blocking the sun to help me run faster. I had been on these very roads about a year ago, driving down from Delhi to Mumbai. But we crossed these roads clocking 100 km an hour in the air-conditioned car and never did get a chance to appreciate the beauty, both in its terrifying and gentle form. I was happy. This is what long-distance running does to you: you discover joy in the simple things of life.

We managed to run 50 km and had a simple, hearty meal at a dhaba. There is a culinary revolution sweeping through our country with Michelin-star restaurants and expat chefs dishing out exotic food. But the Indian highway belongs to the humble dhaba. There is nothing like a piping hot serving of dal chawal at these shacks.

Eventually, after eating our fill, we left for the Deogarh Mahal, where we were planning to rest for a night.

The majestic heritage structure was manna from heaven. After the hardships of the previous days, we were only too thrilled to be in the lap of such royal luxury. The Mahal, which belonged to the Rawats, or noblemen of Deogarh, was well maintained and rather well appointed too.

It was enough to put us in good spirits. Even then we

had no time to sit back and enjoy the creature comforts; we ran from there to Bhilwara and came back only to crash out for the night.

Day 12

We started off on a pleasant morning towards Nathdwara in the foothills of the Aravallis, and on the banks of the Banas river. Nathdwara is famous for its shrine of Shrinathji, which draws thousands of devotees to the beautiful temple.

We ran around the Deogarh village to Bhilwara. It was not an easy terrain, but the undulating green slopes were pleasant to the eyes. There were myriad birds and peacocks everywhere and without the human cacophony, my ears were alive to the bird calls. I saw more varieties of birds on this stretch than I could ever count or identify. Neither could anyone else. In Mumbai, other than the large crows, pigeons and the occasional kite, there are hardly any birds left to watch.

The weather continued to test us but nature was more than willing to compensate, it seemed. And I was lucky to spot a dancing peacock with its plumage spread out in full glory. Thrilled to bits, I called out to the other runners to catch a glimpse of the spectacle, but by the time they arrived, the bird folded its fan and the show was over. It occurred to me that it had put up the performance for my eyes only.

I felt an inexplicable connection to the bird, in just the way that I was suddenly alive and awake to every little thing around me. Was it because of my loneliness during the run?

I wondered.

Running alone did give me solitude. I was always running with just my thoughts and me and was looking for companionship in everything around me—egrets, peacocks, my crew car. In fact, the call of the peacock became my call to fight and a symbol of blessings. Even when I was entering Vasai, much later when the Greenathon was down to its last leg, I had heard the peacock call out, the distinctive sound rising above the din of the vehicles. I knew instantly that it was a sign that I was being watched, cared for and blessed.

But the spiritual experience I was going through was a far cry from the physical hardship of my immediate environment.

Nathdwara was no different from other pilgrimage sites of the country—crowded, dirty and polluted. I wonder why we insist on saying 'Cleanliness is next to Godliness' when most of our shrines are so inhospitable and dirty. I am sure God moved out of these shrines a long time back.

The stretch now moved from the silent and the reclusive paths to the dusty highways again. It was a single-lane road with unmanageable motorists.

The crew and the drivers were trying their best to shield us from the traffic. But it was getting difficult for them to do so without holding up the entire traffic. We decided to start running early the next day and stop only in Udaipur to make up for the bad session.

Day 13

Arvind woke up early. It seemed as if he hadn't slept at all. He was all packed. I was sad but unlike last time, I didn't try to stop him. I was learning to manage alone.

The day's run was over a difficult stretch.

As we started getting further and further from Nathdwara, the roads became more scenic again.

These were idyllic conditions for my asthma.

I saw a text from my husband. He had taken the same route to the airport and texted about the beautiful scenery and the majestic Lord Shiva's temple.

The prospect of reaching Udaipur was a huge motivator for all of us. It would mean we had reached the significant halfway milestone.

I was nostalgic about Udaipur, a place I had visited with my family seventeen years back. The text from my husband just sweetened the deal. The tough running conditions simply seemed to fire me up.

I always love running on slopes, because for every upward incline, there is a downward incline. Since I had had enough practice on the slopes around my house, I was super-confident while tackling these slopes in the open. As we crossed another uphill stretch, I was greeted with the majestic view of the Ek Linga temple, an ancient shrine dedicated to Lord Shiva.

The glimpse of the temple from a distance was enough for me to decide that I simply had to go inside.

The other runners were way ahead of me. If I wanted to stop over at the temple, I would lag further behind. But the desire to visit the temple was getting stronger every second and I eventually gave in. I informed the crew about my decision and they were obviously unhappy about it. But as usual, I stood my ground and they very reluctantly gave in to my demand.

By the time we reached, the temple gates had shut. We had to wait for fifteen minutes for them to reopen. The crew members went off to buy flowers for the offering, while I waited with Pritam, my driver, who rarely spoke to me.

'Once again you will be left behind,' he said, haltingly. 'As always.'

Finally, the man who had thrown a tantrum some time ago was talking nicely to me. And this would eventually be the ice-breaker in our strained relationship. Over time, I came to understand that Pritam's cut-and-dry interactions with me were a reflection of his bosses' attitude towards me. That day, for the first time he made a friendly overture. And I was grateful to him for making the effort.

I offered to take him inside the temple with us, but he politely declined.

'I shall pray for you,' I said. 'Today is a special day for me because you have spoken to me for the first time as a friend.'

He simply smiled and said, 'Now you quickly finish your prayers and come back. I should not be talking so much.' He made it evident that he was on duty and that there were a few lines he wouldn't cross. And I respected that.

Around 10 a.m. the mighty gates opened. The sun was glowing in the skies and Lord Ek Linga revealed himself in all his magnificence to me. My mind went blank. I did not know what to ask for; success, glory—none of these things seemed to matter. I failed to ask for anything personal, but for some weird reason I wanted to climb Mount Kailash, the abode of Lord Shiva. Was it impractical? Maybe. But after I had experienced such intense pain and mental agony over the last few days, I could not bring myself to ask for anything that would seem petty.

I stepped out of the temple, feeling calm and serene. The world around me was beginning to change when I started running towards Udaipur again. I also realized the crew's attitude was changing towards me. It was finally becoming easier to run without any snide remarks coming from them.

As I reached the outskirts of Udaipur, it was Pritam who broke the news to me. 'Ma'am, you have crossed 750 km.'

I was halfway through and the next 750 km didn't seem impossible. I lay on the roadside and dozed off even as the others reached the hotel. The hot tar was so relaxing and I was just too happy that we'd done 750 km in thirteen days.

Once I reached the hotel, I freaked out when someone told me we were staying next to a graveyard. I started chanting mantras to ward off evil spirits, something that everyone found just too amusing. It turned out to be a huge ice-breaker as my driver and crew too started laughing and warmed up to me.

I also took the opportunity to analyse their situation. We

were running during the onset of the Indian summer across some of the hottest states when temperatures swung from 22°C to 42°C in a day's time. It was frustrating for them to crawl behind us at a snail's pace, without the AC on, providing us with food and water.

I was running because I wanted to, and was dealing with every setback with a positive mindset. But for the crew, it was a decision imposed on them by their seniors and they were constantly fighting their misgivings and unwillingness in these inhospitable conditions.

But the halfway mark seemed to change the dynamics between us. They seemed far more civil towards me.

I smiled at the crew and said, 'Congrats, we did it. We have completed 750 km—though we still have long way to go. Thank you!'

They smiled back, 'When do we start in the evening?'

20

Crippling Blow

BAD ATTITUDE, GOOD hotels. That could sum up what the crew had been giving us all these days.

If it was the Holiday Inn in Jaipur, Heritage Hotel in Kishangarh, Hotel Man Singh Palace in Ajmer or the majestic palace in Deogarh, it was the Sheraton in Udaipur to stay. Since this would be the last luxury hotel until we reached Mumbai, we loved it even more.

I was proud of myself. I had finally done it along with the men as an equal. I questioned myself about why I was doing it. I realized that I was doing it for myself. It was my passage of self-discovery. I was lucky to get such an opportunity. All the pain and injuries I had gone through showed me there was an up for every fall. It was strange how, even though we were being put up in lavish hotels in Rajasthan, we never got a chance to enjoy them. I remember our stay at the majestic palace in Deogarh with Arvind. Under different circumstances it would have been a romantic stay for us—with the pool and the luxurious rooms and the impeccable service. But it seemed as though our perspective had changed. Luxurious rooms, air-conditioning, a swimming pool and good food did not really seem attractive anymore. Certainly not as satisfying as running on a cool, cloudy day, breathing in clean air, eating a simple meal of dal khichdi and sleeping on a bed at the end of the day...and laundry service!

Being on the highways for days, and living the way we were, we could not even think of doing our own laundry. We kept piling up our clothes till we reached the next good hotel—especially after experiments with smaller hotels and their laundry service, that resulted in shrunken, discoloured clothes.

I changed and went to Milind's room for lunch. Milind was developing pain in his ankle while Mahesh and Raj were recovering from their pain. Sajjan and Apurba were thick-skinned so were spared from the misery. I always wondered, how would it have been if I was also as thick-skinned like them?

We all discussed our running experience. Every day we all had nothing to talk about other than our runs. How and what was going on while we were running. What were we thinking? Our world was like the equator revolving around the run.

Meanwhile, the bond between us was getting stronger with each passing day spent on the road. And now with the halfway mark achieved, we were celebrating as if we had already reached the finishing line. After lunch I went to my room. I called up my parents and Arvind to tell them about my run. My father was still cautious.

'What you have done is good. But now the real challenge will begin. Don't get overconfident or distracted. Get rest and get ready to run,' he said, the voice of sober reason in the midst of my euphoric celebration.

I lay in the bed thinking about the 750 km I had crossed. I reflected on the past few days; I was proud of myself for achieving the feat of running shoulder to shoulder with the men. And I realized I was doing it for no one but myself. It was my journey to self-discovery and I was lucky to have been given such an opportunity.

We decided to run in the city in the evening, so that the message of our effort to save the environment reached out to more people. This time, there were a couple of runners who joined us from Ahmedabad.

The trail, which went around the Fatehsagar Lake, was beautiful, and we ended up running for 15 instead of 10 km. The lack of vehicular traffic around the lake made it a pleasurable experience not only for us but for our drivers as well, who were only too glad for the break.

At the lake, we were accosted by several curious people. Mostly it was Milind who was mobbed by his fans. The attention and the adulation helped us spread the message of the urgent need and the importance of saving the environment.

I, of course, had my own take on it: 'Save women if you want to save the environment.'

Day 14

I got up at 3 a.m. and requested for crew support. They were definitely more empathetic towards me now. I felt confident and took off my handkerchief from my face for the first time in days.

The highway dust and pollution had made it difficult for me to run without having to deal with the inevitable asthma attacks. But I was now able to run faster as I could breathe easier.

By the time the other runners joined me, I was already far ahead. For once I was the one waiting for the others to catch up. It felt good. Especially when all of them noticed my improvement.

Milind was all smiles, 'You were running pretty fast today.'

'After many days, I was able to run without any breathing trouble. You guys inspired me to run harder, as I was always trailing you guys.' I couldn't help but add with a wink, 'From now onwards, you will have to catch up with me!' Milind started laughing.

After the congratulations that I got from Milind for my rediscovered vigour, the crew too, was left impressed. They had written me off completely and I had had a remarkable turnaround, it seemed.

'I feel good; let me run a little more today,' I told Raj when he came around to welcome me back.

'I feel the same way. We should let people know how badly pollution is affecting us. You should cover a little more today because in Ankleshwar you will have problems running. It is the most polluted city in India,' Raj advised me.

Uh oh! I did not want to be rushed to the hospital again. But I also understood what Raj was trying to say and in the evening, when everybody was still resting, both of us decided to run ahead.

We started well, but a few kilometres later, I began to feel a new kind of pain behind my left knee. Since I was on a running high, I ignored it. Every time it became unbearable I dropped to a walk, and once it was manageable, I started running again.

After all that I had endured, this would be a cakewalk, I thought. But I made yet another mistake in brushing it aside.

We finished running 20 km and I rushed back to my room to apply muscle relaxants and put ice on the affected area. I must have dozed off, because I was woken up by the ringing telephone; it was Raj and Apurba, who were calling me for dinner. But the moment I tried to get up, I felt a searing pain in my left knee. I was suddenly very scared. I was not sure I could go through another emotional upheaval. I felt cheated, but I pulled myself together. I applied more muscle relaxants, changed and headed out for dinner.

When I told Raj about the pain, he asked me pointed questions and concluded that I had developed a stress fracture in the muscle behind my knees.

'Is it serious? I can run, right?' I was getting very worried now.

Raj replied, 'It is not serious. Typically, you would be advised rest to get back on your feet in a day or two. But I don't think you will take even a day off...you can run, but it will be very painful and healing will take more time.'

I chose to hear what I wanted to hear, ignoring the rest.

The last advice from Raj before I left for bed was not to run the next day, but walk, as the injury would get aggravated, and affect my running style.

Just before going to bed, I told the crew to be ready an hour before the usual time. It was a war and I was going to fight it.

21

Widening Cracks

Day 15

We were to run towards Himmatnagar in Gujarat. By now, the temperature had crawled to the 40-degree mark and the humidity was at 55 per cent. My knee was still hurting, but it was manageable. I got ready and started my run after a very liberal dose of muscle relaxants.

Even they had stopped working. As soon as I started, I realized that my rhythm was just not there. I was finding it harder and harder to run, and soon I found myself unable to take another step. I started cursing myself loudly. I could not lift my left leg; my knee hurt very badly.

I walked and limped.

Apurba came up to me. 'What's this? New style of running?'

I replied, 'My knee hurts…I can't lift my leg.'

Raj, who was running alongside, shouted, 'Stop running and just walk. Else you will worsen it. Why don't you ever listen?'

I didn't want to be behind again. I tried to explain something which didn't make sense, still hoping he would get convinced, 'It doesn't hurt when I run. Only when I walk.' My words seemed to infuriate Raj, who snapped, 'Stop running right now! You will ruin your running style and destroy your knee.'

I relented. 'I will run and walk like earlier days,' I assured them as they ran ahead.

I was livid with myself for getting back to square one, just when I was beginning to run well. Today I could not control it. I was heartbroken.

I stopped and fell on my knees, and started weeping. I yelled through my tears, 'Why me, God, why me? Why do I have to suffer so much pain?' I lay on the road crying, curled up in a foetal position.

The days of struggle against my health and the frustrations of the run had all come together in a tidal wave of emotion that was sweeping through body as I lay there. I wanted to run with the others…I wanted to be strong. I felt as if nature did not want me to run.

A little later, Pritam the driver walked up to me and stood there, giving me an icy stare. He did not utter a word, but just stood there, giving me silent company before walking back to the vehicle. I looked at the vehicle and realized I was not alone...

Garmi sardi ka ehsaas badan per rehne do,
Apne mann ko tann ki sab takleefain sehne do,
Apne kaanon ko sab shor sharaba sun'ne do,
Apni zubaan ko saari sachi batain kehne do,
Apni aankh ke chashme mein sab manzar behne do,
Palkon ki is raah ke sarey kaantey chun'ne do,
Apni zaat ke pathreeley aur banjar-pan mein saad,
Umeedon ka garam aur meetha chashma behne do.

(Let the feel of summer and winter remain on your body,
Let your mind suffer the agony of your body,
Let your ears hear the sounds of chaos,
Let your tongue speak only the truth,
Let your eyes see what they have to see,
And pick the thorns that litter the way,
On the lonely and rocky road of life,
Let hope blow warm and sweet.)

I looked up to the impossibly blue sky—there they were, my guardian angels, two white egrets, flying over me. My ears picked up the call of peacocks. The universe was sending out signals to me, telling me that I should get back on my feet and hit the road.

I kissed my legs, my hands, and sent out a silent prayer to

my body: 'Please be with me. We are almost through...once I finish the run I will take care of you.'

I pulled myself together and started running. I was limping but I did not stop—I kept telling myself that I would walk after 45 km. I fixed my gaze on the road, not looking in any other direction.

I reached the hotel, as always, more than an hour after the others. The heat and the exhaustion had completely killed my appetite. But I forced myself to drink some milk and joined Raj and Apurba, who looked pensive.

Caught up as I was with my own struggles, I did not see how things were panning out with the others. Even as I was building my own bridges with the crew, the rift between them and the other runners was widening.

Both parties used me as a sounding board, but did not want me to get involved, so even though I tried to intervene, both the crew and the runners kept me out. The runners were exhausted and unhappy with the mismanagement; the crew members were unhappy because of the lack of support from their management.

Things were now turning nasty, with the crew becoming ruder towards the other runners, especially Raj and the others who had joined the run to support us. The crew was not providing water and food supplies to the runners who were joining to run with us.

Milind was doing his bit to support our runners, but the crew people could not be changed. Seeing the situation, Milind realized that the crew would not help the supporters who joined us on the way to run with us and he could not stand the dispute anymore. He decided to get some help using his own car and driver to provide support to the runners. However it couldn't be done overnight and we had to wait till Ahmedabad.

Eventually, Milind called for a huddle with all the runners. He agreed that what was happening to those who had come to support us was wrong. But he seemed averse to the idea of an all-out confrontation with the organizers, especially when we were only halfway through. He announced that his driver and car would join us from Ahmedabad with the only purpose of supporting the guest runners.

We welcomed the news, especially Raj, as he had already started putting together a list of people who were keen to run with us from Ahmedabad to Mumbai. A confrontation was averted but there were still murmurs of dissent for allowing the crew to get away so easily.

In the evening, we were told that two more runners would be joining us around 8 p.m.

I was very sceptical and told Raj, 'Do they know what to expect? Our crew cannot help them with water and food supplies. They bought stock only for the six runners and not for the supporters. I hope there won't be any further issues.'

'I have already informed them,' said Raj confidently. 'And I hope the organizers do not create an issue again. Besides, they will be staying on their own and they'll manage their water and food.' However, I was not very convinced.

Day 16

I woke up feeling better, even though my body was aching. I took my time getting ready, taking enough precautions before the run.

My driver and the crew member assigned to me now carried enough ice and fruits for me. I also bonded well with the other members of the crew, and was especially happy to see Raj smiling at me as I walked, instead of running.

By the afternoon, we had reached Himmatnagar.

We had our lunch in Milind's room. We were hovering around the 900-km mark and the next target of 1,000 km was suddenly just a couple of days away.

The two new runners brought us news from the world outside. But the evening also brought me back to the harsh reality of the Indian highways. Himmatnagar was crowded and dusty. The pollution levels were also markedly higher. The handkerchief was back on my face again.

22

Life Is Unfair

Day 17

The two new runners, Varun Joshi and Kavin Kondabathini, had joined us to spread the message.

Today as a larger team, we crossed the Tropic of Cancer.

Though, as Raj had predicted, my running posture was badly affected, when we reached Gujarat and saw the stretch of concrete that lay before us, we were very happy—it was all wide roads and flyovers. But we soon realized that the beautiful roads did not really improve the driving of the motorists, who did not believe in conforming to the traffic rules. Vehicles sped at us from wrong directions, stopped in the middle of the road and what seemed to be a perfect stretch turned out to be veritable minefield.

It took us a lot of effort to reach Ahmedabad. We still had another fourteen days to complete the remaining 550 km, equivalent to running a full marathon a day.

Reaching Ahmedabad proved to be a killer. The incredibly polluted air, the heat and humidity was wreaking havoc on our minds and bodies. When we finally reached the state capital, we were overwhelmed with relief and jubilation.

During lunch, Raj and Apurba were telling stories of the last year's run. The hotel we were putting up in was the same hotel these runners had stayed in last time.

The men were celebrating as though they had already finished the run. It was quite surprising because I was still stressed out about the distance and what lay ahead. But for the other five runners, it was all familiar territory.

During lunch, when Milind addressed us, he chose his words carefully. 'We know what lies ahead. Reaching Ahmedabad was the tough part and we made it in good time and in pretty good shape. If we want, we can finish well under thirty days,' he declared.

There was more. Raj announced that in Ahmedabad and Surat, several guest runners would be joining us for day runs. The scars of the previous days paled in significance when we thought about the milestone that awaited us the next day, when we would cross the 1,000-km mark.

In the evening, I chatted with Raj and Apurba as they reminisced about last year's run. They had run 557 km from Ahmedabad to Mumbai for the same cause and with the same runners, but the crew was different. The two veterans recalled how the previous year's crew was more efficient and courteous, which was the reason why they had agreed to be a part of this year's challenge. Unhappy as they were with the set-up this time, the thought that they were running on familiar territory now seemed to give them confidence, and they seemed more relaxed.

But I saw something was eating at them—they were all missing their families.

They didn't get teary-eyed or emotional, but I could easily make out from their conversations just how much they were missing their families.

Before we retired, Raj had a few words of advice for me, 'Sumedha, you better walk rather than run in the evenings. You are limping and if you don't do something about it, it will develop into something serious.'

Apurba joined in, 'Limping is inevitable at this stage, so please change your running stance before it is too late.'

I had nothing to say other than nod my head.

It was not that I was limping by choice. It was my body's response to the pressure on my affected knee. But I convinced them that I had started to change and would improve in the coming days.

We had a surprise visitor in the evening. Himmat, who had joined us in Udaipur, returned today in the avatar of a crew member to support the guest runners. Having experienced the challenges of a day runner in our midst and the noncooperation of the crew manager, he wanted to help the newcomers. He also bought me a pendant of Shirdi Sai baba as a blessing for me, and I could not have asked for more.

Himmat was an ordinary guy, who ran in borrowed running shoes. He joked about the global fad of running barefoot and how he did it out of compulsion and not choice.

Talking to him made me thankful and humble. After thirty days, I would go back to my comfortable life but his reality was very different. Himmat was an inspiration for me.

The evening also brought us a new runner, a woman, Ritu, who accompanied me on my walk. Ritu turned out to be the surprise package—she brought homemade wheat pasta, dal and rice for all six runners. Since homemade food was available after so many days, we ate furiously and silently.

Day 18

I woke up with a huge swelling in my left knee; it seemed that despite showing signs of healing, my knee had just taken a turn for the worse.

Today was a big day for the entire group—this was the day we completed 1,000 km. Fifteen runners were going to join us for the run on the Ahmedabad–Anand highway.

Just before the start, I asked the crew to provide me with a new can of muscle relaxant. I knew the day was going to be pure torture for me. I started slow and in a short time, I was back being alone on the road with the crew vehicle, even though there were so many of us running.

But I forged ahead, constantly chanting to myself, 'This too shall pass.'

My aim was to complete the daily quota and cross 1,000 km. As long as this could be achieved, everything else would be worth it. I put a crepe bandage on my knee and I ran with a limp.

The Ahmedabad highway to Anand was strewn with plastic and other waste piled high along the road. It was a bad day for me and even though I finished 1,000 km by the afternoon, I was not in any shape to enjoy the milestone.

I fainted when I reached the hotel, to resurface only after somebody had sprinkled water on my face, and I puked as soon as I came around. I was feeling extremely weak, so much so that I needed the support of the crew members to walk to my room, where I just crashed.

I woke up in the evening with a bad headache. I had eaten nothing since the morning, so I ordered a sandwich. I called up Raj to check up on the evening plan.

He told me that he, along with some of the others, had knocked on my door a couple of times but had received no response. I must have been extremely tired not to have heard! He told me their plans for the evening and I joined him and Apurba for a run to Sabarmati Ashram. After what we had been through, the ashram seemed like an oasis of peace.

There, Himmat produced another flattering surprise for me. While we were there, he slipped out and returned with a miniature replica of Gandhiji's charkha. As he handed it to me, he said, 'To the girl who is running alone despite being injured. Hope you always remember me.'

I was speechless at his gesture and learnt an invaluable life lesson. It's not the run itself but how I conduct myself with my fellow runners that will define me as a person. I had to be a better person, earn goodwill and spread it as generously.

But by the time we reached the hotel, my head was splitting. I popped a few pills and looked at myself in the mirror.

I couldn't recognize the person staring back at me. I was tired, in every sense of the word. I just wanted to give it all up and go back home. I wanted to put my head on my mother's lap and listen to the stories she told me whenever I was sick.

I felt alone. I wanted someone to hug me and console me and just say, 'Everything's going to be all right.'

I did not have the courage to call up my husband or my parents. I knew I would break down on the phone.

This was my journey, my struggle and I had to face it on my own.

As I lay on the bed, wondering what to do, my father called me. He never called me so late in the evening. How did he read my mind?

'How are you dear?' I could feel his concern and love in his voice.

I just said, 'I'm fine.'

He continued, 'Hope I didn't wake you up. I went into your room today, and I was looking at all your old pictures. You know, you were always different from others. You never listened to us, always fought your way to doing things your way. You were quite a handful!'

We both laughed at this.

'I know, Papa, and I am very sorry,' I said. It felt odd to hear myself laugh...I had forgotten how it sounded.

He was quiet for a second before continuing, 'Don't be and don't change. You were headstrong and always knew what you wanted to do. It is because of that you are able to survive and continue with this run.'

I laughed again and said, 'I guess I am thick-skinned.'

'I know you will not tell me what you are going through... you don't want us to worry about you. I don't even know if I can handle knowing what you're going through. I want you to write it down, I want to read it and feel it. We are very proud of you. Remember the road ahead is going to get tougher, but don't you stop till you reach 1,500 km. You have keep moving forward and keep smiling.'

I couldn't say anything more than just, 'Thank you, Papa.' And then I asked him to do something that seemed just right for the moment, 'Can you sing me a song, Papa?'

My father obliged instantly, no questions asked. '*Hum honge kamyab...hum honge kamyab ek din...man main hai vishwas, pura hai vishwas, hum honge kamyab ek din...*' (We shall overcome, we shall overcome someday. Oh, deep in my heart, I do believe, we shall overcome someday...)

I could sense his voice getting heavier with emotion. He stopped and said, 'It's late Chinu; you must go to sleep now.

Goodnight, my child. Just remember, nature is with you.' Tears were flowing down my cheeks. I did not care to stop them. I sank down in my bed and wept before drifting into a deep sleep.

Day 19

We spent the day running around Ahmedabad and discovered, to our dismay, that parts of it were unbelievably polluted and dirty. There were open garbage dumps and the heat was not helping my asthma either. For all the glorious success story of the city, the ground reality was something very different.

As the mileage was decreasing our daily running miles had also decreased. We now just had to run the daily required mileage and reach the next city. Our mileage was divided into two morning run and evening run.

I decided to take better care of myself, so that I could not only finish stronger but also turn out to be less of an inconvenience to people around me.

By this time, my swelling and the pain had come down. I tried walking and running, and after a couple of kilometres, settled down to my own, if somewhat peculiar, rhythm.

By not taking any breaks, I was able to catch up with the other runners. But destiny had other plans.

I had been reducing my intake of water during the run to avoid going to the toilet. My mother's words of advice at the beginning of the run had completely slipped out of my mind.

Today, it was time for dehydration to wreak havoc. I started getting blisters on my toes, some of which were massive. I had to slow down again. I could see the other runners gradually disappearing from my vision. I stopped and took off my shoes. The only way ahead was to puncture my blisters. I went about rupturing them with a safety pin. I gritted my teeth and went about the task, even though I could see the driver cringing. He muttered a prayer for my wellbeing and went back to the car.

Puncturing the wounds punctured my rhythm. I dragged myself on. What made matters worse was that it was a cloudless sky, with not a speck of cloud to offer me shade.

I entered Anand in the afternoon; Raj and Mahesh had reached forty-five minutes before me. I was tired, hungry and thirsty and wanted to reach the hotel at the earliest.

But on the way to the hotel, something amusing lifted our spirits. We spotted milk booths and immediately stopped to grab a quick drink. Drinking milk straight from the bottle—some of us had six bottles each—brought out the child in us. We laughed and joked about how as kids most of us hated having milk, yet now it tasted like a gift from the heavens. Our lives on the road and on the run had definitely changed something in all of us.

Day 20

As I neared the 40-km mark, I saw a dead python by the road.

On our epic run across the states, I had seen many road kills, including human carcasses. I never quite had the stomach to get used to it. When you are running, the sight doesn't pass you by quickly but takes time, and the stench of decaying flesh follows you.

It made me philosophical about the futility of a life without purpose and the finality of death. There is no difference between a dead animal and man by the road, expect the fact that sometimes the dead man may get a funeral. But a life that is lived without making a difference or making a mark does not deserve a funeral. Each one of us, in our brief time on this earth, is given a chance to make a mark, and unless we do that we all die an animal's death—by the road, a rotting mass of flesh that disappears into the earth and is soon forgotten. It motivated me to do better, run stronger, so that I left an impression on the earth I tread. Time was running out. We entered Baroda in the afternoon; I reached two hours after the others. The heat and humidity in Gujarat was taking a serious toll on all the runners, not to mention the depressing sight of litter, mounds of plastic, discarded bottles and other rubbish that we knew would take decades to disappear, if at all. But the knowledge that they had completed the same course last year gave the veteran runners confidence to continue undeterred.

In the evening we ran inside the city. By now, support, blessings and wishes were streaming in from all over the country.

I also noticed that Raj looked unusually happy. Apurba told me he was glowing because he was about to meet his family in Surat. I wished silently for Arvind to be there for me as well.

Day 21

With a lot of trepidation, we reached Ankleshwar. I didn't want to run and started walking as I didn't want to get breathless due to the pollution. Thankfully, I was not alone; one of the guest runners was also with me.

The air in Ankleshwar was thick with exhaust fumes and chemical gases. Rivers and lakes were all dead, with only stagnant pools of polluted water and more effluents being dumped into them. I was not prepared for this. I was also told that companies offered lucrative packages to employees here to retain them. I found it hard to accept that parents actually subjected their children to this environment, just for the lure of more money.

My nose began to bleed, and I rushed to my room for a round of nebulization as soon as I reached the hotel. I looked out of my window and all I could see where crowded streets and chimneys spewing smoke. I wondered why people were indifferent to this monstrosity.

I met the nephew of one of the guest runners, Varun.

The child was asthmatic and while chatting with the two of them, we came to know that Ankleshwar residents are plagued with chronic diseases of the skin and lungs and there was a high incidence of cancer as well. I also found out, to my considerable surprise, that Varun's nephew was especially interested in meeting me—to be inspired by how I had overcome my own condition to run the race. I was touched and happy to have been able to make a difference in a young life.

Later, while we were in the lobby overlooking the coffee shop, we noticed distinguished-looking gentlemen dressed in their fine suits. They were probably the senior managers of the Ankleshwar factories. The educated man is more dangerous than the illiterate one. He is the reason behind the large-scale destruction of nature and the human race because he wants to make money at the cost of anything. Development and progress cannot be at such a high premium. There has to be an ethical way of ensuring wealth is created for everyone without destroying our world.

I saw an Englishman sitting by himself. I smiled at him and asked him if I could join him. He was surprised and welcomed me. I must have looked completely out of place, walking into the hotel's coffee shop in running gear.

He acknowledged it by asking very politely, 'You don't look like a corporate person. Are you here with your parents?' I laughed and told him that I was part of a six-member team that was running from Delhi to Mumbai, a total distance of 1,500 km in thirty days to promote environmental awareness. He looked suitably stunned to hear that and continued, 'You mean to say that you ran from Delhi till here? Wow, that's amazing! How many kilometres have you covered?'

I replied, 'A little over 1,200 km.'

'But you look very fresh, not tired!' he said.

'Oh that's because I just bathed and got into fresh clothes.'

He laughed and said, 'I am privileged to be sharing a table with such an accomplished personality. Unfortunately, I have not been following the local newspapers else I wouldn't have asked such banal questions. You guys must be the face of the nation these days.'

I didn't know what to tell him, the bitter truth about remaining unknown while creating history was something we had been struggling to cope with.

I said, 'We have not been covered by the local media. There is some coverage of our team leader appearing on a national TV channel. But we are doing our bit and promoting the message through Facebook. We don't have too many followers but some supporters have been coming to meet us on the way and are joining us for the day runs.'

He seemed to understand our condition and remarked, 'If you were doing this in Europe it would have been so much bigger. But what you guys did was a start; it is always more difficult for the frontrunners. May the others who follow you in the future have a better time and opportunity!'

I felt awkward about talking only about myself and asked about him and his profession. He was part of the senior management team at one the world's biggest chemical companies.

I blurted out without thinking, 'So you are part of the topmost polluting companies in the world…'

He looked shocked and took a minute before replying, 'Lately, we have been doing a lot of work to protect the environment as well as make changes in the production and processing units so that we can reduce the amount of pollution.'

'Thank you, sir, for taking these initiatives. I am sure the next generation will have better living conditions and fewer diseases,' I replied. We finished our lunch in silence. Before he left, he asked if he could take a picture with me so that he could share my story with his friends and family back home.

In evening, despite my misgivings about Ankleshwar, I quite liked the Joggers' Park in ONGC colony, the town's tiny green lungs. We were running, interacting with people in the well-laid-out stretch, when I met a young girl and her friends who looked at me with some curiosity. I stopped to smile at them, but was not prepared for the assault that followed. 'Why are you wearing such skimpy clothes?' she asked me point-blank.

I tried to explain that since I was a runner, these were the clothes that would help me run my fastest. But she and her friends did not seem convinced.

They pointed at the other runners and said, 'That uncle is running very fast. You should run like him.' I smiled and nodded at them. But they were not quite finished and had one more piece of advice, 'Stop wearing clothes like men and dress like girls.'

I did not know what to say, but felt sad to see that even an industrial city that was home to multinational corporations, people have not let their children grow out of the box. It was disheartening to see girls being brought up with such prejudices about what they should or should not wear. Her looks become her identity and she is conditioned to judge others by the way they dress.

I kissed and hugged the little girls and continued with my run. But my mind was running faster than me. I was still not able to believe how such a young girl could be so bothered about looks. When I was a teenager, I never knew what fashion was. I got my ears pierced just before marriage. All that my parents taught me was to never give up in whatever you do and show the world what mettle you are made of. They never stopped me from wearing anything that I wanted. Had they filled up my head with such nonsense I would not have been here, doing this, after getting married.

After the short run, when we were chilling in the park, Apurba announced that his wife was meeting him in Surat. My heart silently cried out for Arvind again but I knew that for him to fly down to meet me again would be heavy on our wallets.

But that night, Arvind called. After a brief chat he said, 'See you tomorrow. Goodnight.' And he disconnected. I was at peace.

Day 22
12 May 2012

We started our run from Ankleshwar towards Surat.

We had finished 1,255 km. The thought of meeting Arvind today propelled me on.

I was happy and confident. I felt that we had crossed the biggest hurdles of our run and it was going to be a sweet stretch ahead. Our destination seemed real close.

The journey was now coming to an end, but something new and unpleasant was rearing its ugly head.

With more and more people joining us for the run, the

tussle with the crew became worse. While the new set of runners had been informed about the issues with infrastructure support (or lack thereof) and were self-reliant, when we ran, we did so as a team. So when the supporters ran out of water or essentials, they would instinctively turn to our crew for help. The lines between 'them' and 'us' were getting uncomfortably clear.

Standoffs were frequent with the guest runners who were refused drinking water on many occasions.

Despite the difficulties though, my excitement increased by leaps and bounds as we neared Surat. Apurba was also running with a big smile on his face. Raj was already running with his wife Jyoti, who had joined us the day before in Ankleshwar.

Finally, we reached Surat—the diamond capital of the country. Three of us were going to be with the people we loved.

I was running as strongly as I could. I wanted to show my husband that I was doing well and that I could finish the run without any issues. But I also knew that my posture had changed and I was limping.

After the run, when we reached the hotel, all I could do was to fall asleep in Arvind's arms.

23

Ugly

Day 23

We decided to finish the run before 20 May. Next morning as the distance was less, we decided to finish the run before 20 May 2012.

Milind shared information with us: 'On the City located in Goregaon East to the Yash Raj studio, located in Andheri West. The distance is 10 km.' 'We will have to wrap up on 20 May as required by the organizers. So we can finish 1,500 km in the next couple of days and keep running till 20 May to keep the cause alive.' A large number of runners from Surat joined us. I was happy to see several women in that group. But though we started well, my bad knee started acting up again.

Arvind called up one of his friends, Mehak Choudhry,

in Surat, who picked me up to visit her father, who was an orthopaedist.

Dr Rajiv Raj Choudhry examined me, asking me every now and then, 'Does it hurt here? Do you feel any pain?'

'I don't know,' I said finally. 'My definition of pain has changed.'

'Well, I'm afraid you might have developed a stress fracture. I will be straight with you, child. Do you want me to look into what exactly is the cause or just help you deal with the pain?'

'I don't want to know what is wrong with me. I just need some support to ease the limping and make running less painful. I'm almost done with the run. I just want to finish it,' I said impassively.

The doctor gave me some compression socks, calcium and vitamin tablets and suggested I use Vaseline on my feet for the blisters. He wanted me to get new shoes as well, which thankfully, Arvind had already organized.

'I want you to keep running,' he said before letting me off. 'Don't worry about your pain till you cross the finishing line. My blessings are with you. But promise me that you will visit a doctor and rest and heal before you start running.'

I had no words to thank him enough. 'How much should I pay you?' I asked him.

He smiled, and said, '1,500 km!'

I was waiting outside the hospital while Mehak and my husband were at the chemist's shop. That's when I saw a young girl with no legs, sitting on a wheelchair. She kept looking at me, so I went over to say hello. She smiled and said, 'Are you an athlete?'

'I'm a runner, but not good enough to be an athlete.'

'I used to be great runner too, but I lost my legs in an accident. But soon I will also start running again.'

I was surprised to see the confidence and faith of that girl. I asked her, 'How old are you?'

She said proudly, 'I'm eleven and will be twelve soon...still a year less to be a teenager.'

I could not stop smiling at the way she spoke. She was smart and full of confidence. I wanted to ask what had happened to her but I did not have courage to do so.

But the girl continued, 'Soon, they will fit me with artificial legs and I will also be walking and running again in a couple of months. I am excited but I'm worried also. Will I ever have a boyfriend?'

Little girls will be little girls after all... 'You don't need someone who will love you only for your looks; you want someone who loves you for who you are,' I told her.

The girl looked thoughtful. 'Hmm, I know, but still, no guy likes me anymore. Everyone just pities me.'

'Some day, you will be a woman that every man desires. Just wait for that day.'

'Can you pray for me so that I can be normal like you? You have beautiful legs.' I gave her a hug and said, 'May God bless you.' This was the second time in a row that I had met girls who talked about nothing but physical appearances. It made me resolve to do my bit to bring about a change in the way society teaches girls to look at themselves. They had to be shown that life was not just about looking good.

Day 24

I woke up in the morning and saw that two new runners who had joined us—Kshitij Sharma and Aishorjyo Ghosh—geared up in the lobby to run with us.

Now we were ten people running towards Valsad.

The medication was proving to be effective and I could run without the sensation of pain slowing me down.

Now that we had only a couple of hundred kilometres left, there were many conversations that had to be tied up. How we will finish? What will we do on the last day? What will be our pace and strategy? But one thing was sure—we all wanted to now experience more than just our old lives.

Some of us were feeling sad that we were about to clock our daily quota well before thirty days.

Milind laughingly asked Sajjan, Mahesh and me to save some energy for the last 10 km—our last day's run to the channel's studio in Mumbai.

Thanks to the media blackout, we were actually not interested in going to the studio. All we wanted was to culminate the run and go home. But in the end we all agreed to Milind's proposal.

But now we wanted to push ourselves even further—and were interested in doing more than 1,500 km.

We reached the town of Valsad in the afternoon. Without the pressure of deadlines, we were feeling liberated and ran without any pressure.

Day 25

We reached a beautiful local school in Valsad, Atulya Vidyalaya, where students, teachers and other staff members, including the principal, joined us for the run.

I followed my run-walk routine. I was getting better but did not want to push myself more than required. It was a very pleasant day and we finished 35 km in the morning.

The principal of the school was extremely meticulous and we were greeted with an amazing spread of sandwiches, biscuits, chips, tea and plenty of water.

Typically, whenever we reached the hotel, this fare was the first thing we were served. The only thing missing was cold coffee, given that this was a school.

The crew, however, had done their homework and had organized cold coffee. But only for Milind.

When Raj asked for some, they refused him flatly. 'It's for Milind, not for you,' said the crew manager. Things started getting unpleasant with Raj blowing his top and exchanging barbs with the crew. But since we were all in a school, we tried to calm down the warring factions and not make a scene in front of the children.

On our way to the hotel, I hoped that we had seen the worst of it, but little did I know that something much worse was about to happen.

Raj was not quite done.

The moment he reached the hotel he confronted the crew again.

I had no idea what exactly went on behind the closed doors, because the next thing I was told by Apurba was that Raj was packing up. I couldn't believe it.

Apparently, the crew manager had complained about Raj to the organizers and Milind was supposed to ask Raj to leave the event. I rushed to his room. All the other runners were there, except Milind, who was in his room talking to the organizers, trying to resolve the issue.

We all begged Raj not to leave. We urged him to swallow his pride, because he had already made so many sacrifices and we could not let the organizers have the last laugh. We wanted him to finish and stand proud in front of everyone. But all our efforts were in vain.

Raj's heart had been the proverbial straw that broke the camel's back. Milind tried somewhat to convince the crew manager but was not very effective.

Meanwhile, Milind came back after his conversation with the organizers and said quite impassively, 'Raj, you behaved like a kid. If you are facing a problem, you should tell me. Why did you have to lose your cool? Abusing cannot be forgiven. There was no need to pick a fight with the crew...for them we are nobodies.'

Raj stood his ground. 'They were rude and I was not

wrong in standing up to them. I lost my cool because I had had enough. I'm not going to apologize.'

Milind may have understood his point of view but it was also obvious that he could not defy the orders from the organizers. 'They want me to ask you to leave,' he said with an exasperated shrug.

We all were quiet, tense…till Raj spoke up. 'Can I run?'

Milind patted him on his shoulder and said, 'Yes, you can and you should. Anyway, you don't need a crew. You can have my car. We are running for the environment, not for the crew. So relax and let's run.'

We decided that Raj would continue to run and finish his 1,500 km. But he would leave the hotel and join the other runners from Mumbai to finish it.

In the evening, we started our run towards Daman.

From a distance, I looked at the entire group running and wished that things were back to normal. Deep inside they were all wounded. I never thought this race would be so much more about the mind than the body.

Things had changed very fast and for the worse. Gone were the days of merriment; instead, it was all about stony silences between us.

I couldn't sleep that night. I kept wishing that all that had happened was a bad dream that I would wake up from. I prayed for everything to return to normal. I didn't want to call up or talk to anyone, so I put on my iPod till the time I drifted off to sleep.

Day 26

I woke up, got ready and went to lobby for the pre-run coffee and snacks. I saw Apurba sitting all alone and then it hit me cold and hard...Raj was not there. Apurba was downcast as well. He wanted Raj with him. For days, weeks, they had shared the same room, run shoulder to shoulder, encouraged each other and shared their triumphs. It was all gone now.

Before we started, I tried my luck and apologised to the crew on Raj's behalf. But they just turned their backs on me and asked me not to interfere. I felt lost.

As the run started, we saw Raj and the other new runners. I was happy that at least he had company.

Eventually, we all started running with Raj, with Milind's car following him. But it seemed as though he had lost his will to run. His mind had shut down and his body was also slowly shutting down. But we never left his side. It was also very endearing to see the support runners sticking with him and we became his crew for the day.

The only question that came to my mind was whether this race would end on a happy note. After 20-odd km, we started walking on the highway.

24

End of the Dream Run

Day 27

Mornings were no more the same. We did not have tea or sit together in the lobby. We just got ready and went out quietly. It seemed everyone was avoiding each other.

The support runners had their own difficulties, their own challenges, like the rest of us. But no one ever asked them if they needed anything or how they felt about it. Two of them—Varun and Kavin—decided to go back to Mumbai the next day. I wished I could stop them but by now, the situation had gone beyond that.

We reached the hotel with a heavy heart when I got a call from Raj. He wanted to meet me separately outside the hotel to discuss something important.

I went down and saw Raj engrossed in a discussion with Apurba. For a second, I wished it was just like old times—that I was joining them for lunch after the morning run. And that everything was just the way it used to be. Unfortunately, it wasn't.

Raj had made up his mind. He wanted to quit and leave for home. Apurba and I frantically tried to dissuade him, but he just would not listen. We were all just another day away from completing 1,500 km.

We really didn't want him to throw it all away at this stage. I called up Raj's wife, Jyoti and told her briefly about what had happened. She assured me she would talk to him and join us tomorrow to resolve things. I felt better.

After the evening run, during which I felt an impenetrable wall had come up between us and the organizers, I requested Sajjan and Mahesh to take up cudgels on Raj's behalf. But they did not want to interfere. I made my way back to the room with a heavy heart; I realized this was Raj's fight and he had to fight it on his own.

Day 28

We left for Vasai. We had lost our health, lost our peace and now we were about to lose our minds too. I skipped lunch after the run, hoping to be left in peace. By the evening, things had become worse. No one said much. But a few runners who had come for Raj decided to run with him to complete the run. Those were the longest hours of our lives. Forty-eight hours of pure hell.

Just before we could start our evening run, my mother called up. 'How are you? I know it is an odd time to call, but I know you are close to home and we will be reaching Mumbai on 19 May. We cannot wait to see you…best of luck for the last bit!' she said encouragingly.

'Mama, things are very hard. It's not ending the way it should.'

Like all mothers, she panicked. 'Chinu, is anything wrong with you?'

'No, I'm fine…I just don't feel like coming home and at the same time, I am missing home. These beautiful days are getting over soon.' I wish I could tell her what was happening, but I did not want her to worry.

Her daughter had been running on deserted roads and dusty highways for nearly thirty days. Soon, she would be reaching the all-important milestone. I did not want to take away from my mother's moment of excitement, joy and pride. I owed her this much.

She kept consoling me, 'Stop thinking so much. Just go with the flow. Sometimes obstacles come in the way for a reason…for a new beginning.' I smiled. I had my answer. Yes, it was my new beginning. A new me.

I called up Arvind at night as I was not able to sleep. He was surprised to get a call so late in the night.

He sounded worried, 'Why have you not slept?'

I replied, 'Nothing… I will be completing 1,500 km plus tomorrow. I'm ahead.'

'I knew you would do it! But why are you awake? Go to sleep, and I'll see you tomorrow,' he said, keen to get back to sleep and get me to rest as well.

But then I dropped the bomb. I told him that I was coming home the next day. He was suddenly alert and wide awake.

'Are you serious?!'

I told him about all that had happened today. I had hinted about it earlier in the day, but even he was appalled when he heard about the fiasco.

I had decided to go home the next day to be at peace with myself and get away from the ugliness and muck that was staining the beautiful thing we had created over the last few weeks. This drama was not what I needed in my life. 'When I culminate the race on 20 May, before my family, I want to be all smiles, not brooding,' I said to Arvind, as he heard me out—patient and understanding as always.

One of the biggest lessons of endurance running is tolerance.

For far too long we had been slugging it out in the polluted environment, on the poorly maintained highways that turn into killing fields thanks to irresponsible motorists. It tested us so much and kept us hyper-alert all the time, thinking only about survival and finishing on good time, that we had no bandwidth to bicker among ourselves. We simply took everything in our stride and moved on.

When you try to achieve something extraordinary, it comes at a price. And this fallout between old friends and comrades was the price we all unwittingly had to pay. Ideally, we should never lose sight of the target and accommodate all the negative elements in the best possible way.

It would have been easy to say that the weather was inclement and blame the bad organization every time we were injured or close to quitting. At every step we were being tested—our beliefs, our endurance, our faith, everything. Every now and then we would ask ourselves whether it was all worth it. Each one of us had fought our individual battles and now it was time for us to go on.

I said goodnight and promised my husband that I would go to sleep. I closed my eyes and started thinking about my family. Then I got out of bed, took out my purse and looked at their photographs. I was glad that I was born to a regular family, which had made it easier for me to achieve this feat.

Contrary to popular perception, I believe it is easier for someone from humble origins to make it big rather than the children of eminent parents. For a nobody, there is no pressure, no comparisons, but only glory for those who dare. There is an innate drive to achieve and turn out to be exceptional. However, for the child of a famous parent, the first fight is to get away from the comfort zone, step away from the shadow of a famous surname and sweat it out. But there too, a lifetime of comparisons await, with hard-won achievements being eclipsed by the overwhelming presence of the famous parent.

I lay on the bed, feeling proud about myself. Today all that mattered was me.

25

I, Me and Myself

Day 29

Today was going to be our last day on the road before we entered Mumbai. When we started running, we all ran as one. We crossed the borders and reached the city. The joy and exuberance was missing but there was a feeling of relief on everyone's faces.

At lunch we all celebrated for the last time, but the celebrations were definitely subdued.

In the evening we crossed the 1,500-km mark. For the last time I lay on the road that had been my home all these weeks. I looked up at the sky.

I saw my past and all that I had been through flash before my eyes. I saw a car pass me by with a family in it. I saw a kid, and thought how I longed for my own. Conflicting emotions were sweeping through my mind. A month ago, all I cared about was this run. Nothing else mattered. And now, after all that I had willingly and unwillingly put myself through, I desperately wanted to be a mother.

With that urge came the nagging doubt—what had I done to my body? Would this body ever be able to bear a child? I had just ruined my breasts and my knee and my asthma was worse than ever. How would I raise a child? I realized the damage I had caused my body would take a few years to heal. I would not be fit for motherhood at least for the next couple of years.

On the other hand, I was not happy. I mean, I should have been elated now that the days of sheer physical torture and mental agony were coming to an end, but I wasn't. It seemed that in the 1,500 km, I had moved from being a girl who wanted to be more than a woman, but in the truest sense, all I wanted to be now was a mother.

There was so much I had to talk about that I felt choked with all the unspoken words. I just kept looking at the sky and tears flowed out—of joy, of sadness, of anger and pain. I felt a surge of sympathy towards myself. I just wanted to hold my body and nurse it back to normal. I kept rubbing my hands on my belly imagining how it would have felt to be a mother. I had also discovered the most beautiful and precious thing—myself.

After a while, I looked back and I saw Pritam standing

and watching over me. I smiled at him and got up to leave.

He stopped me and told me something very memorable, 'Madam, this journey has not finished. The path is very long. You will meet a lot of people who will envy you and talk trash behind your back. This is just a start and you will have to do much bigger things in life. Do not let emotions come in your way. Listen to your heart and mind and not the voices of those around you.'

Even if Pritam intended to warn me about something sinister, I was not prepared to listen—because to listen or pay heed to a warning would have ruined the special moment I had just had with myself.

After the evening run, I went back to hotel where we were staying to pack my stuff to leave for home. Milind and Apurba had already packed for home. It was a feeling of joy and at same time of grief. As if we were bereaved.

The journey had ended but I wanted it to go on. This is what I wanted to do for rest of my life. I knew that, but I had to work for a living. This would be a journey I would always cherish.

I went to my crew vehicle and caressed it lovingly. It was my last day in the vehicle that on many occasions had been my life saver, and the sole and quiet witness to my tears and laughter, my little victories and defeat. 'One day, I'll own you as you were my friend in need. Thanks for never making me feel I was alone,' I said to the car, running my fingers over it.

Despite all that had happened, I had developed a great

bond with the crew. I could not have achieved the milestone without their support. I met each one of them to thank them.

The crew leader said, 'We never wanted to hurt anyone and we did everything to the best of our capability and ability.'

I replied, 'Thank you all. It wouldn't have been possible without your support. We might had our differences but I will always be indebted to you.'

As I took their leave, the parting words of the crew leader kept coming back to my mind: 'We never wanted to hurt anyone...' I looked at Apurba and thought about the other runners of our team.

I realized that the morale and bond of the team was broken and was affecting everyone. The fellowship was dissolved and we were all headed our separate ways.

I packed and said goodbye to everyone. The crew arranged our travel; it would be a short run tomorrow in Borlivali's Sanjay Gandhi National Park, with Mumbai's running crowd.

On my way home, the realization that the run was ending hit me. Mumbai is notorious for its traffic snarls. Getting stuck on the way back home was the final wake-up call—I was home; I had made it.

Arvind was waiting for me on the road, below our building. I had never seen him more excited.

I entered my home. It looked just the way I had left it. But I missed my comrades waiting for me there, as they would after every run. It was finally over. I looked at Arvind and started weeping.

I had achieved everything I had set out to. But it was also supposed to be a team effort. And that's where we had failed.

We went out for dinner that night. My husband had chosen a fancy restaurant to celebrate my success. When I walked into the restaurant and sat down, I felt odd. I had got so used to having dinners wearing my running gear on—which sometimes was all sweaty and smelly. While I was dressed up for the occasion, in my mind, I was still wearing my shorts, T-shirt and Nike shoes and I was looking around so that people wouldn't stare at me. My husband looked at me, smiled and pressed my arms to calm me down. He just asked me to relax, clear my mind and have a good time. We had a quiet dinner; my mind was filled with so many thoughts I didn't know how to express. My husband updated me on what was happening on social media. He went on to talk about the increasing support for our run and the storm it had kicked up regarding Raj's situation and eviction. He also mentioned that at the next day's run at Sanjay Gandhi National Park, Raj would be there to run with us. Even though he was not a part of the team, Raj was still running with us as an independent runner.

But I was not so sure. At night, I called him up. Raj assured both Arvind and me that he would be there. Even then, I tossed and turned all night, unable to sleep on my own bed.

Day 30

I woke up at 2 a.m. as was my usual routine during the run and got ready. Arvind was asleep. The run in Mumbai was scheduled to start at 7 a.m.

I still had enough time and I went down to the sea and sat there for a long time, until Arvind woke up. I watched the sun rise over the Arabian Sea and thought of the many sunrises that had kept me company all these days. I watched the ebb and flow of the water and thought of the many tears and laughter we had shared as a team.

Later, we drove to Borivali National Park. We travelled in silence, lost in our own thoughts.

'Everything will be fine. All of you will come together today,' Arvind assured me. I fervently wished that would happen.

The social media was abuzz with the harsh reality of the run. There were scathing remarks from the incensed community of runners about the treatment meted out to all of us, except Milind. The angst and the resentment were spreading like a virus.

How could everything be all right? I wondered.

26

The Last Mile

THE SANJAY GANDHI National Park was buzzing with runners when we reached. The crew was there too.

I looked around for my comrades. Apurba was the first to arrive with his family. Mahesh and Sajjan were also soon in our midst. Milind joined a little later. We were all chatting and joking around but Raj had still not arrived. I kept an anxious eye out for him.

I was relieved to finally see him arrive. I gave him a look of gratitude as we took our position and got ready to start.

After the run, we were all together, including the crew, having refreshments, when a few members of the Mumbai Marathon Runner's group asked Milind about Raj. Everyone was aware of the dispute between Raj and the crew, thanks to the social media.

Milind was calm and composed when he replied, 'Raj was and is a team member. The crew had asked him to leave but the team did not. We ran as a team and will end as one.'

His answer cleared the air.

So many people kept asking me about my experience. I still struggled to find the right words. The journey had not yet finished for me.

Arvind, in the meantime, had left me to pick up my parents who had flown down just to see me complete the race. They arrived by the time we were done and I was overwhelmed with joy when I saw them. I wanted to hug them tight and cry, but since we were in such a crowded place, I restrained myself.

On our way home, Papa and Mama had the same question for me—how was the experience? I felt lost. I didn't know where to start.

Till that day, I had told them that everything was fine. But today I would tell them the entire truth. My parents were even more eager. 'Papa,' I said, 'I will make you listen to the song that I used to listen to every day when I ran.'

Ruk jaana nahi tu kahin haar ke,
Kaaton pe chal kar milenge saaye bahar ke.

(Do not stop, defeated only by treading on thorns will you get to the pleasures of springtime)

The music was the answer. There was only silence as we made our way home. I looked outside the car window and all I could see was buildings and vehicles. I was disheartened at the idea of getting back to the rat race. We were all running after things we could never take along to our graves. And when we did run 1,500 km for environmental awareness, most people in India knew nothing of it.

At night I called up Raj to check on his plans for the next day. Raj was still upset and unsure of whether he should join us for the run the next day at the TV studio. I had one answer—he had to. No one would stop him.

'It was a team effort and such small issues always crop up when you battle the odds as a team. Had it not been you, it could have been any of us. When people come together under such circumstances, there will be tears and laughter. One should look forward to the smiles and ignore the fights,' I told him. Raj reluctantly agreed.

By now, all those who were following our event were supporting Raj. But still he felt alone, isolated and alienated. He wanted his friend Milind by his side; nothing else mattered.

Day 31
20 May 2012

I was up again at 2 a.m. When I went to the kitchen to make tea for myself, I saw that my mom and dad were also awake.

I went to their room, anxious. 'Why are you awake so early?' I asked them, wondering what had gone wrong.

'We know something is bothering you,' said Mama, patting my head. 'You should always speak your mind. It eases the burden.'

I smiled weakly. 'Mama, trust me, it's nothing...just that I cannot come to terms with the fact that the run has ended. I can't seem to adjust to my home.'

'Chinu, we expected you to be happy and smiling after achieving this feat but you seem to be indifferent, distant... which is so unlike you,' said my mother.

My father added, 'Chinu, when we walk and run alone we usually forget the world we come from. But we must accept the real world and apply what we learn from our journey to our real life. Inspire, learn, be thankful and be open-minded. I don't know what happened on this journey but I would like you to pen it. You must share the experience with the world.'

'I'm fine, Papa, but somehow, I'm not happy,' I mustered the courage to say.

I didn't know what else to say. I diverted their thoughts by saying, 'I'm missing nature, the highways and my team. I never imagined I would get so attached to all of it, that ending the journey would hurt so much. From tomorrow, I will be a slave again, running behind paltry increments. The world will judge me on the basis of my salary and the car I drive. But I'm not worried about the judgement. I'm ready for it.'

My father said gently, 'You make us proud. I'm happy you found the truth for which people seek gurus and yogis. Nature has shown you the light. You are lucky.'

I offered to make them tea and we decided to walk down to the promenade to catch the sunrise together.

I did not tell them about my anxiety. I was worried about how our run was ending. I still hadn't told them about what had happened in the last few days.

Gradually, I felt like I was getting back to my old, chirpy and positive self. We chatted till the morning. I was eager to hear about all that I had missed in the last thirty days. By the time Arvind joined us, we were all looking fresh and happy.

We reached Film City, based in Andheri, right on time; it was from there that we were going to be shot running to the studio of the media house that had organized the event.

I wanted this run to end just as it started. I just wished that Raj had been there too. We had a few Mumbai runners also running to support us. I noticed the crew was also behaving very differently today. They were happy and smiling as today, the epic and tumultuous event was getting over. Whatever the reason, I was glad.

Everyone except Raj was there. Apurba had come with his mother, wife and daughter. I was there with my family, Milind had his close friend Rahul Bose and fans with him, Mahesh had his friends and coach and Sajjan had us as his family.

Thankfully, Raj arrived just a few minutes before we had to start off.

We runners held hands and said, 'Let's do it one last time.'

We all were almost in tears.

We ran together for the last time together, just as we had done on day one. As usual, I was with them for a few kilometres, then started lagging behind. But I loved every step of it.

When I saw them running ahead of me, I felt complete. My dream had come true. We were going to end the Greenathon just the way we began.

Epilogue

THE THIRTY DAYS of the epic run had irrevocably changed something in all of us. But now, we were all back to our quotidian lives, nose to the grindstone. It was tough, as most of us did not really have a choice. But the camaraderie we shared has survived over time.

After the Greenathon, Raj Vadgama continued with his interior design business but he also combined his love for the great outdoors, his skill and his passion, to launch a fitness company. He now runs a fitness academy in Mumbai, 'Xtreme sports'. His son is an engineering student and Raj and I continue to remain close friends.

Apurba Dass went back to his railways job but still runs like a Ferrari. His wife is better now and his daughter is a student at Sophia College. He and I are now close; our bond seems to have gotten stronger over time.

Sajjan Dabas went back to working with his father and

runs whenever he gets time. We still talk once in a while and have developed a great deal of mutual admiration and respect.

After Greenathon, Milind Soman started his own event, Pinkathon, which is a multi-category running event for women. It is held annually across various cities in India to spread awareness about breast cancer and women's fitness. Milind and I continue to remain friends.

Mahesh has not been in touch with me, Raj and Apurba. I don't know where he is and what is he doing but I heard he got married. I'm sure he will be happy in his new life.

As for me, the run of my life was proving to be far more challenging than the 1,500 km that I had run in thirty days.

Instead of appreciation and encouragement, all I heard was criticism—why was I so slow?

Voices of dissent and discouragement within the running community kept saying, 'Sumedha is not good runner. She is very slow. She was not as fast as others. Why did she even sign up for the run?'

There were no laurels or bouquets for me, as the community that I had strived so hard to be a part of, seemed intent on questioning my abilities. But honestly, I did not need their validation anymore. Running the way I did, under the circumstances, had taught me one important thing—to turn a deaf ear to criticism.

There was a silver lining, though. When most people were busy talking behind my back, there were some who looked up to me as their mentor. On 15 August, 2012 I was felicitated in

Amritsar. Several colleges and corporate companies invited me to deliver motivational speeches. My graduation college, DAV College, Amrtisar, honoured me and invited me to mentor the students. It was redemption.

I was back in office on 21 May 2012. I had exhausted my quota of leave and I did not even take an off to get my knees checked after they had faced the brunt of my ambition. Things did not look so good on the health front. I had developed a stress fracture, so I was off running for four months and kept myself fit by combining yoga and walking.

The office environment was turning out to be more dissatisfying every day. I simply could not connect with my job anymore. Money, fancy designations and promotions were completely meaningless to me now. I was sure I was killing myself over something that was utterly insignificant.

Unable to come to terms with my vacuous work life, I put in my papers in October. I took some time off for a bit of soul-searching. I came to the conclusion that after having discovered my individuality, I was not prepared to squander it away, toiling to fuel other people's ambitions. I wanted more than just salary and promotion. During this time I started preparing my next big event. In December the same year, I ran for a twenty-four hours event completing 152 km, which is a new national record for women. After looking at the records under my belt in one year my confidence got doubled. My faith and belief in myself grew stronger. I realized that one dream which I always had but, until now, never had courage to do was to start my own business strategy firm. When I expressed this desire to Arvind, I knew he might not agree with it but I still gave it a try. As expected, he said, 'It is a big risk, we will have to liquidate all our savings. This way we can never plan a family for next five years. It is too much risk and our life is anyway full of debts and commitments. It is not wise. You can do it after a couple of years once you have more experience. In the mean time I suggest you go back to work. It's just because you are idle you're thinking too much.' I agreed to him and took up job in a financial company in January 2013. I was back to old life. But life never works as per our plans.

In February 2013, I injured my lower back once again. I had a slipped disc and an oedema in my sacroiliac joint. My life changed. All of a sudden it was upside down. I had to quit my job, motherhood again took back seat and above all, running was gone. I was on bed for months and with ceiling to look up. I was broke and sadden. But I had no time to rest and brood over the miseries. I learned life is uncertain and I have to make most of it. I decided to follow my dream—my dream to start my own business strategy firm.

As expected, my decision created quite an uproar in the family. Everyone objected, saying I was taking a massive risk all over again. I went to one of my entrepreneur friends in Mumbai, to seek his advice and support. But when I shared my plans with him, he bluntly discouraged me saying, 'Sumedha, you are just two years old in Mumbai. You don't even know half of the places here. Starting a business is too much of a risk and that too in the field of business strategy. You should start with freelancing and then after a couple of years graduate to establishing your own firm.'

His words did warn me but my mind was set. I had to do it now or never. I started my treatment for slipped disc and with the help of Dr Abhay Nene, a spine specialist, and physiotherapy, I was able to regain much of the lost ground—and my confidence. I was excited and all geared up. I started doing research for my business plans. Having my own firm will give me more time to recover faster and become better runner.

In April 2013, with the support and guidance of my friends I started my own venture, Karta Business Consulting. I proved all of them wrong again.

Karta Business Consulting is a marketing and business strategy company that helps the senior management in companies to solve their most important business problems. We believe that we can help improve business performance, not only at companies plagued by inefficiencies but also at otherwise healthy companies by helping them reorient themselves in the turbulent business environment. We are a professional services firm specializing in providing support in the areas of business/marketing strategies and management training programmes.

Today, Karta Business Consulting is catering to companies across India. It is a small firm. Yesterday it was a dream but today it is reality.

As far as running is concerned, because of my firm, I was able to take out time for treatment and get back in shape for running. It took me eighteen months to get back to running, but now there isn't any looking back. I was back on track by the end of August 2014 and now I am eyeing bigger targets and longer distances—motherhood can wait for another day.

My journey and struggle continues but I am not deterred. It only makes me more determined to work harder.

Live your dreams. Follow your heart. Do not give up, no matter how many times you fail. Life is all about getting up and not going to sleep till the time your dreams are achieved. There is no tomorrow, today is all what matters.

Take a leap of faith and follow your dreams. The dreams which you had forgotten as societal norms bogged you down. Go and create your own MILES TO RUN BEFORE I SLEEP.

Acknowledgements

First and foremost I would like to thank Sri Shirdi Sai Baba, for always being by my side and helping me reach out for my dreams without fear.

I would like to thank my father Dr. Vishav Bandhu, who asked me and encouraged me to write my journey. Without his push this book would have never happened. Thanks to my husband, Arvind Prabhakaran for being a rock of my life. He has always supported and motivated me to follow my dreams. Without his support and encouragement this book would not have been possible. Thanks to my mother Dr. Kamlesh Gupta who inspires me to be bold and beautiful. Thanks to my sister Mrinalini Misra, my brother Keshav Mahajan and my brother-in-law Abhishek Misra who are my best friends and who have stood by me in thick and thin.

I'd like to thank my grandparents for allowing me to follow my ambitions throughout my childhood. Thanks to my extended family, including my in-laws who have always supported me and I really appreciate it.

I would like to thank Milind Soman and Raj Vagdama, for giving me an opportunity to be a part of Greenathon; Pratik Acharya for helping me with registration for my ever first marathon (Standard Chartered Mumbai Marathon); Kanishka Gupta for helping me in the process of selection and Chandrima Pal for helping in the process of editing, you guys are simply awesome. Thanks to Rupa for publishing my story.

Last and not least, I beg forgiveness of all those who have been with me over the course of the years and whose names I have failed to mention.